MYSTIC GUARDIANS

JAMIE HAWKE

Editors
Diane Newton
Tracey Byrnes

MYSTIC GUARDIANS (this book) is a work of fiction.

All of the characters, organizations, and events portrayed in this novel are either products of the author's imagination or are used fictitiously. Sometimes both.

WELCOME

Want to never miss a new release, stay up to date on what's going on, and get a silly little spiced-up "Building Your Harem Guide?"

SIGN UP HERE

WARNING: This book contains adult content. A lot!

If you'd like to keep updated on new stories, freebies, and recommendations of other stories I admire, come check out my FaceBook page at:

https://www.facebook.com/JamieHawkeAuthor.

Thank you for reading!

All the best,

Jamie Hawke

M y heart still hadn't stopped pounding from the intense lovemaking I'd just had with the ladies while Sekhmet had watched, and now it was in overdrive with the idea that I was actually about to go train with King Arthur himself.

Or, his ghost? I wasn't sure what exactly he was in this land, as he'd been sort of sacrificed and we thought gone, but then he reappeared only to tell me it was time to begin my training. Nivian—A.K.A. the little mermaid, A.K.A. the Lady of the Lake—had said he was a spirit, that he'd been sacrificed by Morgana to bring back Merlin... who was apparently not on our side? It was all so confusing.

"What could that mean?" I asked Sharon, darting past her and the others, stuffing my mostly still erect cock into my pants as fast as I could and trying to find my shirt. "Training…?"

"You'll do great," she said, offering me a supportive smile, motioning to Excalibur in the corner, where it leaned against the wall, its metal glowing a light blue.

I paused, turned to give her a kiss, and grabbed Excalibur. There I hesitated again, because she still hadn't put on her clothes. The others hadn't either, and I had to stand there for a moment just appreciating what I had. Sure, the world was in danger of being conquered by Ra and other gods and evil fairy tales, or Legends. And yes, I was in Avalon, or the Fae realm, at risk of dying the moment we returned to Earth.

But all that aside, staring at Sharon's curves, the way Red's large breasts seemed to be calling for me to come over and take her nipples in my mouth, or the seductive way Pucky was staring at me… And damn, Elisa had just turned around to start dressing, inadvertently giving me the view from behind. Yeah, I was the luckiest man alive.

Now wasn't the time for all of that though, as Arthur himself was about to train me. Arthur, who apparently became a vampire due to a curse, was going to train me to be a true Protector of the Myths.

"Tuck away your sword," Red said with a chuckle, and I glanced at Excalibur, confused, only to realize that staring at them my cock had gotten hard again and was sticking out the top of my pants.

"Ready for round two?" Pucky asked. "We can tell Arthur to hold his horses."

I chuckled, but shook my head. "As much as you know I'd love it… save it for when I get back?"

"*If* you get back," Elisa said.

"Hey now." Red hit her playfully. "Don't tease him."

"Is there… a risk of that?" I asked.

"As Nivian said." Elisa winked at me. "Dragons."

I gulped. "I'm… I'm gonna go now, before you all make me change my mind."

I stepped to the door, only then pausing at the sight of Sekhmet with her cat sister on her lap, eyeing me with an arched eyebrow.

"Wait," she said, a hand on my forearm. "You'll be fine. You're the Protector."

"Thanks." I tried to take another step, but the goddess stood and let the cat slink away. Her hand traced my forearm up to my chest, letting it linger there right next to one of the water tattoos that symbolized my tempest powers.

"That's not all." She leaned in, voice a whisper in my ear. "I wanted to tell you how hot you were, when you were fucking, your balls rocking back and forth. Maybe… Maybe I'll talk to the girls, and we see about me joining sometime. Would you like that?"

I gulped, my cock stiffening even more, and all I could do was nod. At least she was wearing her beautiful woman face at the moment, because hearing those words from her when her face looked like a lioness would've been quite strange.

She gave me a grin, walking past as I finally remembered to put on my shirt.

"I'm really doing it," I said, and gave them all one more smile, remembering the tastes of their lips and pussies, the sensation of their flesh pressed against mine, and cumming with them… all very fresh in my mind.

Taking a deep breath and trying to concentrate my thoughts on how terrified I'd felt at seeing that agent reveal himself to be Ra, anything right now to get my focus back on training and off of my amazing romp, I stepped outside to find Arthur and see what he was going to teach me.

2

N ivian was there at the doorway, speaking with Arthur. She gave me a slight nod of the head as I emerged.

"You look like you've already been training," she said, eyeing me intently. "I sensed a spiritual awakening inside, so gave you all your privacy."

I gulped, not sure how I felt about the 'spiritual awakening' being discussed around the king, a true hero of mine, one who I'd grown up loving and reading all about. Of course, I hadn't known about all the vampire stuff back then, but then many did.

"It's perfectly natural," Arthur said, the blue glow radiating off of him almost like a gentle blue flame, similar to what I'd seen on myself back there at the moment of climax.

"Your majesty," I said, not really sure how to behave here, so giving him a Japanese style bow first, then feeling like an idiot and going to one knee.

"Aw," Nivian said, and she had a hand to her mouth. "That's sweet."

"Please, none of that." Arthur motioned me up. "I haven't been a king in quite a long time."

I stood, not sure what to do from there, and nodded.

"I'll leave you to it," Nivian said, and went to enter the house. "Are they… decent?"

"Rarely," I said.

She laughed. "If I tell them you said that, are they going to kick your ass?"

"Most likely." I chuckled, turning back to see that Arthur was smiling, his vampire fangs fully visible. The joking had helped to put me at ease, but that sight instantly set me right back again.

He eyed me, waiting for Nivian to go inside, then said, "Ah, the teeth."

"I don't understand," I admitted.

"Long ago, in another world—quite literally," he paused, chuckled at himself, and went on, "my life didn't exactly go according to plan."

I wasn't sure if he was going to say more, so stood there, waiting. The sword started growing heavy in my hands, Arthur's eyes on the sky as he was clearly lost in a memory. After a bit he nodded, turned, and started walking toward the lake.

Apparently, I was supposed to stay with him, because he started talking.

"The stories talk of Merlin like he was my helper, my right-hand man. They spin him as this wise sage, the ultimate defender of Camelot." Arthur glanced over, blue eyes taking me in, weighing me up. "The truth is that he was a paladin who lost his way, a man who led me to a cursed sword, all part of a prophecy that he, but very few others, knew of."

"The sword in the stone…" I stared at the sword in my hands in amazement.

He nodded. "It was put in that stone for good reason. For when I drew it, the stone carried with it a very dark power. One that sent me down a dark path, and set up me and my knights to serve the former paladin turned sorcerer."

"I'm sorry, your majesty—"

"Just Arthur, will do."

"Arthur…" I was relieved when we stopped, not sure if I should sheathe the sword or keep it at the ready. "I'm sorry, but how, er why, I mean—"

"There's too many questions, too many answers. Today we aren't here to discuss the topic of my past, but to focus on your future. What I will say is that his paladin magic allowed him to have control over us dark beings, and his new magic grew out of that. The Merlin of reality was, and is, as dark as they come."

"So you know, at least?" I glanced around, lowering my voice as if that would change anything. "That he's escaped?"

Arthur nodded. "It's funny, them bringing me back only to send me here again. I'll tell you the rest of my story someday, but suffice it to know I found a way to escape Merlin's captivity, rose up against him, and found my way again. So now I'm here, training the new protector."

I stood tall and proud.

"But that brings us to you, Jack," he added. "Why should we put our faith in you?"

What the hell kind of question was that? Having been through what we had, already having proved myself to Red and the others, I didn't know where to start. Then I remembered what he'd said about himself. It wasn't about my past.

"I've given up my life to do this, and I'm willing to see it through to the end. My end, if necessary. Whatever I've proven to this point, I know it's just the start. I plan on training hard, being devoted to my Myths and the cause."

"Good." He stared, waiting. "And we test that right here, right now?"

"In what way?"

"I'm glad you asked," he said, and then took a step back, then another, until he was on the lake. He was a spirit, or something like that, so it shouldn't have been such a surprise. But then, drawing a blue sword of light, he motioned me to follow saying, "Catch me, fight me. Let's see what you're made of."

He took another step back, eyes taking on a ferocity of their own, before turning and running, darting across the water.

My first reaction was to open my mouth and stand there like an idiot. I couldn't fucking run on water!

But he was going to train me now, apparently, and I was a Tempest... after all. So, I took a step, and my feet got wet.

Damn.

"We're all losing faith here," Arthur called from across the water, halfway to the middle of the lake now.

I glanced back and noticed a couple of heads duck out of the window of the little cottage. It kind of annoyed me that they were watching, but then again it gave me courage. Made me want to prove myself. Not that I was proving how badass I was, but proving my loyalty, that I would never give up.

So I took another step, water cold and up to my ankles with both feet now. No matter how much I wanted it to happen, it simply wasn't.

"Maybe we find another protector," Arthur said, pausing now to turn around and taunt me. I could barely make him out, only a dark silhouette against the sun's reflection on the lake. "Think your team would like that?"

Taunting me wasn't going to work. But something needed to.

I glanced down at the sword, considering it. The Lady of the Lake had given it to me, right? The legends all played with that concept, and here I was at a lake, Excalibur in my hands. Pulling up the blade, I watched the blue glow that seemed to shift within the metal, considering the magic that was within.

Slowly, I lowered the blade to touch the edge of the water, mentally asking for permission to go on, and then took a step up. The blue glow ran up my arm from the blade and filled my body, landing at my feet as the bottom of my shoe touched the surface, and I stood there, bringing my other foot up. With first one step, then another, I was walking on water.

"First lesson," Arthur called out. "It's not always about what you're capable of, but learning to trust those around you, to think outside the box and try new things."

"That sounds like two lessons," I shouted, running now, feeling the excitement charge through my body like currents of electricity. Each step hit like I was running across a massive trampoline, the sword in my hand feeling light as a toy.

Arthur laughed and said, "That's number three—always make sure you learn more than one lesson from an encounter."

Instead of running away this time, he charged me.

When I stepped back, the water started to give way. Fear, apparently, didn't jive with this part of my sword's water power. Keeping that in mind I braced myself, stepping back onto the surface, and charged Arthur.

Water sprayed up around us as we clashed, his sword acting every bit as real as mine, in spite of the fact that it appeared to be made of light. His sword connected with Excalibur and both of us were thrown back, tumbling and gliding across the water in a way that made it feel fun to fall.

Then we were up again, charging forward, and I felt the thrill of the fight, the warm tingling of my

Tempest tattoos coming to life. Arthur leaped into the air, snarling with his fangs extended, and came down with the sword high… Again, the blast hit and we were sent back.

Only, this time he'd been ready for it, and dove under the water to come back up at my side, pulling me down.

"Seems I can't strike the blade that made me," he said, pulling me under so that I lost the ability to respond. He was clearly working my grappling skills now, his blade fading and mine falling from my grip, in spite of how hard I was working to ensure that didn't happen.

My breath threatened to break free, the water pushing down all around me, and then a voice said, "Don't let it win. You and the sword are connected now. Embrace it."

It was his voice, but from inside my head.

I struggled, hating the fact that the lake's surface shimmered above us, darkness all around. Everything in me said this was it, that if I didn't beat him, I'd drown down here. But it wasn't about beating him, it was about learning.

With that thought in mind, I focused on what the situation was. What could I learn? For one, this world was a spiritual one, but still very real. Arthur was a spirit, though, and not himself exactly. I wondered… Not struggling now, but focusing on the fact that it was me against a spirit, and suddenly I was free, his arms passing through me like a ghost. And then I was diving for my blade.

But Arthur whisked around me, taking on the form of the water itself and then Nivian was there in her mermaid form, going for the sword as well. I felt the need for air and started to panic as I saw her mischievous smile. In that crazed state my mind jumped to the worst conclusions, sure she was there to help steal back Excalibur for Arthur, and that this had all been a ruse for that one purpose.

My ladies had made it very clear to me that I needed that sword, that it was part of this battle, and so I remembered Arthur's teaching, about how it was connected to me, and I reached for it, pulling with my mental energy.

In a flash it was flying through the water, blade first and nearly cutting Nivian's tail. It shot up to me and I reached out, grabbing the hilt and letting it pull me to the surface. I emerged and stood there with the sword raised for a moment before I processed the clapping and cheering from my team, now fully clothed and standing at the lake's shore.

Arthur and Nivian rose to the surface a moment later, all laughs.

"Boy, you're a fast learner," Arthur said as he

stood next to me, a hand on my shoulder. Nivian started swimming back to shore, where she stepped out, tail turning into legs.

"I have to be," I replied. "I was thrown in the deep end. Before with Pucky, and now… literally."

"That you were." Motioning back toward shore, he led the way, talking as we went. "I wanted to see what you're capable of, Jack. And I have to admit that you've impressed me. But that doesn't mean it'll be easy by any means."

"Sir—" I started, but he glanced over, about to correct me. "I know, no majesty, no sir? Right. Arthur… Thank you."

"For?"

"You don't know me, you've been around so long and likely met so many people on both sides of the spectrum of good and evil. But you're here, with me, helping me to become a better fighter."

"Not just fighter. Protector. I mean to see that you cultivate your inner core, that you become the greatest version of you that you can be. We'll have you trained up on the blade with Red, magic with Pucky and myself, fighting the darkness with Sharon, and Elisa's protection. In many ways, you have the perfect team." He noticed my frown. "And yet, something's bothering you."

"All this, while Ra and the others are wreaking havoc on Earth."

Arthur smiled, then laughed.

"I don't see how it's funny," I replied, aghast.

"Jack, time doesn't move the same in our world. Does it ever in these spiritual realms? There are pockets of space we can move through, and while it's not time travel, it can slow or speed up how much time we want to have passed, based on where we enter."

"Like portals in the Nether," I said, nodding. "Yeah, I get it."

He frowned. "I don't think it's the same, but yes, for now we'll go with that."

When we reached the shore, the others turned to Arthur anxiously.

"What's the damage?" Pucky asked.

"He's useless other than for a good lay, isn't he?" Red said, but winked my way.

"You've found yourselves quite the Protector here," Arthur replied. "The real test will come when he's put up against the gods, but until then, Shades will have to do."

"Shades?" I asked, glancing around, expecting them to come popping out of the shadows.

He nodded. "Not here though. In the mists. Let's

get you some more training in, then head over. We need your strength and stamina, but especially your speed, to level up quite a bit still. Well, best way to do that in here is to grind."

3

A rthur and Nivian took off not too long after the lake exercise, saying they were going to scout out the mists, look for a good spot for someone at my level—thirteen, and with my current skills. I really wanted to ask him more questions, to spend more time getting to know this amazing figure from history and myths, but knew I'd get my chance later. He was a spirit now, after all, and didn't exactly have anywhere to go aside from being with us, helping me. While they were gone, I'd gotten actual practice with knives and swords with Red, then spent some time with Elisa discussing her woven shirts and other defenses she knew.

We even had a moment to take a break for a

snack, during which Pucky leaned against me and kissed my cheek.

"What was that for?" I asked.

"Because I'm about to kick your ass, and wanted you to know I lo—er, adore you, first."

I arched an eyebrow. Then kissed her back, but this time on the lips, letting it linger, feeling her warmth. When I pulled back, I held her gaze and said, "The feeling's mutual. Remember that, when I kick your ass."

She laughed, standing now. "Come, break's over."

"Where're we going, exactly?" I asked.

Her playful grin and lack of an answer made me very curious, but as we walked she started going on about how we had to take this seriously, how with Ra and the others out there, we were in for some crazy shit. No playing around.

After a few times of her repeating this sentiment, I took her hand and spun her around. "Pucky, I *am* taking this seriously."

"It's just, I don't know… how…" She bit her lip to stop it from trembling. "Too many were lost last time." After a moment of silence, she said, "You've heard of Vasilisa? I watched her die in my arms, felt her ichor leave her body, watched the enemy absorb her ichor!" Her chest rose and fell, fast. "You have to be stronger."

"We won't let that happen again." I actually hadn't heard of that name, but this wasn't the time to tell her so.

She nodded, eyed me timidly, and then said, "We're here. So… sorry for this."

"What're you gonna do?" I glanced around at the trees, the peaceful nature of this place, sunlight flittering through the leaves and birds chirping. It was like being back home, only… better. "Mind control me again? Then what, I have to try and resist?"

Her lip curled and her eyes went green. I'd never seen that happen, and I was about to stumble back, when I caught myself, remembering Arthur's teaching. She cocked her head and tree roots shot out of the ground, whipping me while some wrapped around my legs and arms. The trees were moving like in a thunderstorm and the whipping kept coming along with rocks and other debris.

If not for my shield upgrades and increased defense and health, I'd not only be pissed, but quite possibly dead as well!

"What the fuck?!" I shouted over the roaring commotion, and tried to pull free. I was getting stronger with my stat upgrades from the prana earned to date, but not enough for this. Pucky was damn powerful, and I wasn't sure what my options were here. I'd left Excalibur back at the cottage, so cutting my way out wasn't an option.

Pucky was a Druid class and could do this, so I figured that my being a Tempest could prove useful here, as it had at the lake. Water was everywhere, and that was apparently my specialty, according the tattoos that had formed. Pulling on the water in the sky and clouds, I brought it down on us in a torrential downpour. I tried directing it at Pucky, hoping to get her with a massive tidal wave or something like that, but she stood her ground as more rain did hit her, but nothing like as much as I'd had in mind. Apparently, the powers were limited by realistic forms of the elements. The rain was coming harder than I'd hoped for, actually, but it did accomplish something I hadn't thought of—it made the roots slippery, so that I could pull free.

A flurry of leaves came at me, but only as a distraction while a tree actually swayed down my way! Here I was all action, running and leaping up onto it, then to the other side and rolling. Another was there, waiting, and slammed me back, knocking the wind out of me.

Pucky muttered one more apology as another tree loomed over me, ready to strike. Fuck, this wasn't going well. I tried for the water again, even tried pulling Excalibur, but it must've been too far away or maybe needed the water connection to work like that. Instead, though, as I dodged and strained myself to pull, I felt a new force. A burning formed on my lower right lat, a sensation I'd experienced before when a fresh tattoo was forming, showing signs of new powers.

Wind. It came strong and hard, like me in our little cottage sexcapades. The blast of wind hit Pucky and knocked her off of her feet, even blowing against the trees to push them away, diverting them enough to give me room to stand and run to a clearing. I stood, bracing myself, ready for whatever came next.

Pucky pushed herself up, hands out, and said, "Enough." With an impressed nod, she added, "Not too shabby, if I do say so myself."

I grinned, but was exhausted. Two steps toward Pucky, and I started to collapse. She rushed forward, catching me, caressing my cheek as she said, "I'm so sorry."

"It's necessary." I tried to be strong, pushing myself up. "Let's do it again."

"No need," Arthur said, and we turned to see him and Nivian at the top of the hill, the sunlight shining strong behind them. "We're ready for the mists."

"We should say, the mists are ready for him," Nivian said, and chuckled.

I was starting to wonder if she liked watching me suffer, so stood a little taller, not showing weakness. "Bring it on."

Sure enough, she looked let down by my reaction. Funny. If she could have seen how exhausted and beaten-up I really felt, she'd have been smiling from ear to ear.

4

W alking through Avalon itself, or at least the place the stories were based on, held a special importance to me. All of my life I'd been the type to dream of grand warriors with their swords, fighting evil. Of the fairy kingdom, and the idea that we could be better than we were, that there was a magical place in the back of our dreams that could shine through any of us if we only let it.

Maybe I'd let the fanciful cartoons get to me a bit too much, especially the old-school one about King Arthur being some football captain taken back through time to lead his team with the help of Merlin. My uncle had passed that one down, spent a few good Saturday mornings watching it with me over shared caramel corn and something he said was

a true classic but I never could understand
—Jolt cola.

Looking at the real King Arthur, I wasn't sure
what to think of him compared to the version of
the tales. This man had been a real king a long
time ago, had lived and breathed, had been around
at the same time as Merlin. Only, the sorcerer had
been some sort of corrupted paladin who cursed
the king into becoming a vampire that he could use
like a puppet. It was so mind-blowingly insane, it
almost seemed real, as reality went. That's why I
had no trouble latching on to these stories. If
they'd seemed more grounded, I would have
believed them to be lies. But King Arthur himself
as a vampire? That's too crazy for anyone to
make up.

"I hope you're feeling better," he said, referring to
my little training session with Pucky in the woods.
His eyes moved to Excalibur, now back on my hip
since Nivian had brought it for me, and I couldn't
help but feel it belonged to him.

"Hey, throw me in the Pits of Despair," I said,
hand on the sword's hilt, "I'll come out swinging."

He frowned, looked to Nivian, but she shrugged.

"They aren't as caught up on the movies as I am,"
Pucky whispered, and then added a wink as she said,
"Dementors are so cool."

"Wrong movie," I mumbled, but low enough that she didn't hear.

"What?"

I smiled, nodding, and made a mental note that we were definitely going to have a mandatory movie marathon when we made it back to the real world. Or, Earth... as I guess that place had to be real, too. How could I have been there, otherwise?

"This won't be like last time," Arthur said.

"Last time?"

He nodded. "When Riak pulled you in, I hear. We'll be entering their domain, true, but at that point you weren't fully here. Now that you are, it's much more dangerous, but also much more exciting."

"How so?"

"For one, you know that ichor prana you get to level up your stats?" He waited until I grunted in confirmation. "Well, on Earth let's say you were sipping it through a straw."

"Sipping prana?"

"Stick with me." He motioned to the rolling hills, the thick blanket of fog ahead, or maybe that was the mists? "Here, you'll have the opportunity to do combo-kills. The more of the Shades you take out in a short amount of time, the more linked they are, creating an amplification to the prana earned. No more sucking it through a straw, if you do it right, here you can be thrown into a pool of the stuff."

"You're saying, if I do it right, if I take out Shades in this kill-combo way, I get a bonus." That checked, as the process wasn't so different from various games I'd played. "But then, why isn't everyone out here leveling up and maxing out their stats?"

He laughed. "Because, not everyone has Excalibur, for one. And not everyone is a Tempest."

"What he's trying to say," Nivian cut in, "is that you only have a chance because of what you are, and the weapon you're now latched to. In there, most of us wouldn't stand a chance. We can take them in our world, even outside of the mists, but in there…"

"Imagine it's like lightning," Pucky said, indicating a cloud with her hands. "Now if you're on Earth, there's a thunder storm and you're not so worried. In life, it's not so bad. Go down a slide, get a static electricity shock. Maybe hear about lightning hitting someone on a rare occasion." She took her hands and cupped them together. "Now you're in that lightning cloud, and you're made out of metal—right? Well, as far as this is concerned, we're all metal. So are you, but you're like a lightning rod, made to refocus that energy, to put it to better use."

"That use being leveling up?" I looked at the blanket of fog ahead, seemingly so peaceful. My heart was thumping as my excitement for the adventure ahead rose. "But wait, I'm going in there alone? Arthur, you're a Tempest, too."

"I am, but you'll need me out here, you'll need a beacon to guide you home."

"A beacon? Like a lighthouse for a ship…" I froze, a chill running through me now at that same sight. "You're telling me I'll get lost in there, otherwise why would I need a lighthouse?"

"Jack," Arthur put a hand on my shoulder, "what will happen in there is up to you. But what I can tell you is that it's rife with Shades, ready for the picking. Pluck those grapes, stomp on them until you have the wine of the gods, and then drink up."

A look at Pucky and she nodded, confirming that he was attempting another metaphor. There wouldn't be any actual wine.

"Fight, stick to your instincts, and use your powers when appropriate," she said. "Do that, and you'll be fine."

"And remember," Nivian said, "you're a tempest. Use that shit."

I nodded, honestly still getting used to that part of who I was. My strange tattoos could give me power and help me connect with the elements. Apparently I could do weird things like walk on water, as Arthur had taught me. But how that applied here, I wasn't sure. Then again, looking at the near wall of mist and reminding myself that this was water in the air, I could see how interesting results could come from using powers. Somehow.

Mist started drifting by, slow moving tendrils of it, at first. Suddenly, with a swoosh of color the mists pulled back, swirling, creating an entrance like the cave of fucking wonders. Not so panther like, but there was definitely some sort of animal face look going on. Somewhere between a dragon and a cat.

"Is this thing going to eat me?" I asked, meaning it as a joke, although the words came out sounding very nervous.

"Yes." Nivian didn't even try to hide it, just stared at me, deadpan. "You'll be swallowed up."

"Fuck. Thanks."

Pucky cleared her throat. I turned to see what she had to say, but instead of talking she threw her arms around me. "Kick their asses." She kissed my cheek, then added, "When you get back, I'll be waiting. And I want to see your skills at work."

"I—I'm not sure if you're talking sexually or—"

She hit me, playfully, chuckling as Nivian watched. "No, no, of course not that way."

"You all just had an orgy," Nivian said. "Don't try to pretend you're not a sex-obsessed pack of horndogs."

Pucky blushed, glanced away, and shrugged. "Fine, that too. I'll be looking forward to it all."

I grinned, then turned to Arthur. "So how do I find you, if—you know. When I'm done."

"Or about to piss your pants in fright?" He laughed. "As long as you hold Excalibur here, we're bonded, in a sense. I'm like your spirit guide. Hold up the sword and say, 'By the power of gra—'" He couldn't finish, instead laughing heartily. "See, I know pop culture."

I frowned, really having no idea what he had tried to reference.

"He Man," Pucky explained, seeing my confusion.

"Oh, before my time," I replied.

Arthur frowned. "Don't pretend to be so all-knowing in the future, then. Seriously, though, if you concentrate, the sword will guide you to me."

"Oh, like the Princess Bride!" I said, holding the sword out, closing my eyes and pretending to stumble around like Inigo Montaya when he was looking for the Man in Black. "Yeah?"

He shook his head. "No. I made my one cultural reference for the day. Just… do what I said, it'll guide you."

"Ah, okay." I turned back to the mists, really wanting to delay it longer, but also eager to get my stats up so we could return to Earth and fight the gods and Legends. "I guess this is it, then."

"Good luck," Pucky said.

"Kick ass," Nivian added.

Arthur simply waved, then added, "Have fun storming the castle," and winked.

He might have been locked up here, but at least he knew his eighties culture. I'd have to ask him about that—maybe a little stint on Earth during that time?—but it could wait until I returned.

For now, I had some grinding to do.

5

Stepping into the mists had the exact feeling I'd expected it to—bone chilling unease, mixed with a thrill for the fighting to come. After what Pucky had thrown at me, I wasn't super worried about some old Shades. So I drew Excalibur and walked on, anticipating the fight with tense muscles, breathing heavier than it needed to be.

But nothing came.

At first I was on edge, thinking they were all waiting just out of sight, about to strike at any minute. Some sort of massive Shade ambush, and that I'd been led astray by Arthur. Soon, I stopped caring, more enthralled by the sights of this place. While mostly it was hard to see anything other than the mist, at times it would give way to reveal tall hills, and—when I was lucky—even taller statues. Grand, monstrous carvings of what was at one minute marble, at another gold. They would actually change before my eyes, too, not just from one statue to the next. The perfect reminder that this wasn't my world, and that my understanding of how the world worked meant nothing here.

I passed under one statue that showed a woman's upper half but a snake's sinuous body lower down, the tail wrapping around a hill full of trees. Another stood over me, so that as I passed beneath, I looked up to see its massive stone cock aimed down my way. That was disturbing, to say the least, and I had to think how horrible it would be to stand there in the rain, water cascading off of it as if the giant were peeing on you. How anyone could've ever carved something of this magnitude was beyond me, but then I realized they didn't have to. This was a land of magic, after all.

For a while I walked on, finally sheathing my sword to give my arm some rest. The ground was uneven, in places giving way to small drop offs, so that I had to be careful where I was going. Another statue appeared as the mist gave way, this one like an ancient guardian looking out over the direction I was heading in. Maybe toward something in particular, but the mist didn't allow me to see. Walking past, the mist started to cover him again, but I stared up in awe. He looked like a great king, actually, more than a guard, now that I was at an angle to make out a shape on his head that could've been a crown.

And when I'd walked far enough, I saw what he was actually looking at. Kneeling over a river, wings spread out behind her, was a glass sculpture of a fairy queen. I could almost imagine the light hitting her wings and sending colors cascading through, if any light ever reached this place. A thought that raised the question—had this place once been free of the mists? Arthur spoke of the mists as something to use, a training ground of sorts.

But that didn't mean the land was better with them there, or that once this hadn't been the most beautiful place to ever exist. It was while I was staring at the beauty of this sculpture that I felt the gust of wind that blew the mists to cover her, then the chill.

In a matter of seconds, the mist was so dense around me that I could barely see my hand when outstretched. As I looked at it, something moved out there. Darting. Fast.

"What do we have here," a voice asked. "Walking among us?"

I spun, drawing my sword, and that's when the first attack came. While on Earth and when visiting the spirit realm before the Shades had been mostly nebulous, formless creatures of dark, but that wasn't the case with these things.

This was clearly a Shade, in the brief moment I saw it while the thing charged me and I cleaved half its arm off with my sword. Gray skin that drooped, shadows moving around it as if alive, and then those black eyes. Like the onyx of my aunt's necklace, but less heart-warming. Hands grappled for me, catching me off guard. It took a moment to find myself, to bring my elbow up and then kick it off so that I had room to come in with the sword and finish him off. Another came, then one leaping out of the mist from above—where I assumed must've been a concealed ledge.

By the time the third fell, I had my groove back and was taking them down left and right, glad to finally be doing what I'd come here for. My prana levels were skyrocketing as I found a whole group of Shades, throwing out my group shot skill over and over, and using my magic shield when needed.

When the first group had all fallen, but another was coming from my right, I pulled up my stats and amped them up with new upgrades, seeing then that I still had a skill point from before. I'd totally forgotten about that. I decided to wait again, to see where I'd need it *after* my grinding, as what I had so far should've been plenty for this.

But for the moment, I upgraded strength, speed. When I did, I realized there was more to this than I'd seen before. Maybe it had to do with the level, or my new connection to the spirit world? Strength was now at two-hundred and thirty percent of where I'd started at, speed at one-hundred and ninety. Not bad!

A roar sounded and the Shades were upon me, the first two meeting my sword in the form of a thrust to a gut and then a slice to a neck. A head went rolling, more prana in my system.

On some level, I started to wonder if I should feel bad about this slaughter. After all, back on Earth they'd appeared as basically shadows, not these living creatures. Then again, they *were* trying to kill me, so there wasn't any real reason why I should care.

This was grinding at its best, and because it wasn't just like in the video games, it didn't get to the point where their deaths started to decrease in value. Every upgrade of mine made them easier to kill, but I didn't get diminishing returns of prana. That meant my motivation level didn't falter, the only thing slowing me being stamina.

Seeing as I could upgrade stamina whenever I

had a downbeat, as long as I had the prana to do so, I didn't have much to worry about in terms of staying in the game. More fighting, more slicing, more running through the mists and shouting at them to come back and fight me as they ran.

And run they did. New groups of Shades would show up, but soon I'd either killed all those in the vicinity, or they'd run off. It had been such a relief compared to the lack of action before.

When a pause came, I noticed the chill was gone, and the voice returned. "Ooh, and he's good with a sword, too. We like that."

Another spin, eyes searching, and I stopped as the mist parted to show the glass statue. Had it just moved, or was it the mists around it moving? Both, according to my eyes, but vision could easily play tricks on someone in this situation, so I started moving back in that direction to be sure.

The mist was heavy again and I kept walking, but was certain I'd been going in the right direction. There was no statue, only the river. Even as the fog cleared around me, all I saw was open air.

Strange, but then I heard a thud, looking into the water to see a face looking up at me, something in the water pounding on it as if on ice, but the water was flowing freely. She had no strong features and was transparent, like glass, so that I barely noticed her, then she was gone, swept away with the water.

I reached, too late, then stood and ran along the river bank.

More Shades appeared, but I cut through easily enough, not giving up on the lady in the river. Prana flowed into me and I focused on my mission, adding points to speed as I ran so that I was able to pick up the pace, and then, at a point where the river bent, I leaped in, grabbing for her.

My hand went through the water and she vanished, the mists suddenly swirling in and twisting around me, laughter carried on the wind.

"Oh, he is so chivalrous," a voice whispered, a giggle following.

I spun, scouring the mist for any sign of something, even a shade or ghost. Nothing. "Who's there?" I asked, pulling myself out of the river.

Instead of an answer, a Shade appeared, knocking me back into the river so that Excalibur was knocked from my hands. The water was freezing, my lungs seizing up in the cold, and I thrashed about as the Shade took me, pushing me down.

What struck me more than the cold, though, was the look of this thing in the water. On Earth they had appeared as mostly shadows and in the Fae world as strange, almost alien creatures. Not here though. Here they looked like men, men that maybe they had once been… but with pure, black eyes.

I'd lost my sword, but pulled up my arm in defense as he came in for a strike—it hit as I rolled, pinning him to the rocks at the bottom, shield at his neck. A good yank and then I released it as he vanished, giving up the green prana.

Turning, searching for Excalibur, the green light caught on its reflection. There was that transparent woman again, dragging my sword away from me downstream!

What the hell had Arthur done to me, letting me go into this place? I swam after her, nearly giving up, when I remembered my Tempest training. The water shot me forward so that I had her in my grip, but she slipped away. That didn't stop me, and as I was propelled forward I managed to get around her, hands on my blade, and she was gone.

Rising out of the water, I stood on the river, holding my sword, pissed that I was so cold and wet.

"Who the fuck are you?" I shouted, taking a step onto land and holding my sword out in challenge. "Show yourself!"

A disapproving tsking, then mists formed as the figure pushed herself out of the water, too, walking toward me. Three Shades appeared, but she waved a hand and colorful balls of light appeared, attacking them, so that they vanished a moment later.

The lights came over to her and landed as the mist formed around her body, no longer translucent flesh. At that point they were close enough for me to make out that the light was actually little fairies, and now that they were on her, moving into her, she had more and more color. Even her wings were lighting up, the mist taking color as it became her clothes.

She stood in front of me, arms spread out, and said, "Well, impressed?"

Of course I was, but instead I asked, "Should I be?"

"Honey, you stand before the queen of fairies."

I frowned, thinking how that meant something very different where I came from. "And that would make you…?"

She frowned, waving my question away. "This is my domain, not yours. My house, once upon a time, and you should be telling me what you're doing here. I owe you no explanations." She glanced at the sword. "With that, no less."

Meeting anyone in a place like this didn't inspire the most confidence, so I decided to play coy for now.

"I'm here to kill Shades, nothing more."

Her frown showed she disapproved. "And if you were told to stop?"

"By you?"

She nodded, regally.

"Sorry, but I don't know who you are. Queen... of fairies, yes, I got that much. But... whose side are you on?"

"Are there sides now?"

"You're aware of the war." It wasn't a question, but an observation regarding the knowing look in her eyes. She nodded. "And you haven't picked a side?"

"I have not." She stood, staring at me for a moment, then vanished.

"What?" I said, confused by her action. "That's it?"

Nothing. I spun around, expecting her to show up out of nowhere, to test me somehow, but she didn't return. My body was shaking with the cold, even more so since I was still wet, so I wanted to keep moving. After a few minutes of wandering around the area, even finding an empty cave and taking time out to sit and consider this weird experience, I returned to the grind, searching out and cutting down any Shades I could.

I spent a good half hour after that searching for

Shades, but at the end had only found two, neither of which were much of a challenge.

Applying their prana to strength—figuring more muscle meant more warmth, I said fuck it. Two-hundred and sixty percent strength, now. Still not sure what to think of the whole situation, I decided I'd had enough. There was no way I'd dry off out here with this heavy mist, , and I wanted to ask Arthur what he knew about the fairy queen.

rthur had said to use the sword to find him, so that's what I did. Sword held out, focus on it, I started walking. At first nothing happened, but when I turned a couple of times, in one direction the mists visibly parted and the sword started glowing, blue lines of light moving along the blade.

Good thing, too, because making my way out of the mists proved to be quite the maze. I don't know how I'd managed to walk around some of the hills and straight walls—or cliff faces, it seemed in some cases—but the way back was full of them. If there was a normal concept of time there, I would think it took a good half a day for me to finally get to a point where the mists let up and I could see the trees and hills beyond.

Talk about a relief. Being surrounded by thick mists like that for hours on end starts to wear on anyone. While my recent training and knowledge that I would soon be put to the test helped me through, I was pretty sure that one more minute would've caused me to take my own damn sword and slice off an ear. Or something else equally insane.

I had just made it over to the trees, thinking I'd take a rest there, when I noticed the smell of fire. A moment later I saw the flames, small, flickering pleasantly in the dim light. The opportunity to dry myself left me feeling ecstatic, but I was surprised to see a campfire burning, and at first prepared for the worst. As I drew closer, however, a red cloak became visible followed by a flash of white I'd come to associate with Elisa. Likely some sort of ward.

"What're you doing here?" I asked as I emerged.

"Figured you might want some company when you returned," Pucky said, dropping down from a tree nearby. Her eyes roamed over me and she grinned. "Getting buff in there."

"Thanks."

I glanced around the fire, noting a much larger party than I expected. "Who…?"

"Ah, yes. Let's introduce you." Pucky led the way, with Elisa standing at my approach, giving me a pleased smile, and then gesturing to three men all in white. They looked familiar, though I wasn't sure where from.

When she said, "I'd like you to meet three of my brothers," it clicked.

"How's that… I mean," I turned to them, offering my hand to each in turn. "It's a pleasure to meet you all. But how is it that you're here?"

"It's like Arthur," Elisa replied. "Because they reached a certain level of enlightenment before… being defeated, they're able to remain here."

Arthur grunted at that. "A true blessing." His voice betrayed his sarcasm.

"You're still with me, at least," Nivian said. "I for one would rather that than the alternative."

He offered her an apologetic look, then nodded. "Me too, of course. I just mean, it's a strange sort of existence, being unable to fully operate as a human, unable to return to the real world."

"But this is real," I protested, feeling sheepish for saying so. "Isn't it?"

"In a way."

"And you're not exactly ghosts, right?"

Arthur shared a look with the brothers, one that said they weren't quite sure of the answer to that.

"We don't know what we are," the eldest of the brothers said. "We're vaguely aware when we're called upon for help, though in truth we never leave this place."

"And the other brothers?"

"Off on a quest," the younger brother replied.

"This place," Elisa interjected, "is like Earth, but with a much smaller, and much more magical, population."

"One difference," her eldest brother added, "is the fact that here, magic isn't hidden." He looked at me for a moment longer, then leaned in, voice hushed. "And what are you hiding? What're your intentions with our sister?"

"You seem romantic with more than one of these ladies," another chimed in. "How exactly does that work?"

"I…" Shit, how was I going to explain this one?

"Brothers," Elisa said, and she was glaring. "My personal life is none of your business."

They frowned, but seemed to be okay with dropping it for now.

"At any rate," the oldest brother said, "at the moment, our brothers are searching out a legendary item said to have the power to bring people back from this world to yours. Back from the dead, some say."

I turned to Arthur and Nivian at this, excited at the chance for them to be together again in the real world.

Arthur shook his head at my look, though. "Rumor of anything like that existing doesn't mean it truly does. We have magic, but that doesn't mean all magic is possible. Truly bringing someone back from the dead…"

"But you returned from here once before," I protested.

His voice was much more sorrowful when he said, "That time was different. I had entered of my own will, not… defeated, as I was this time."

I got the implication there—that something similar had happened with the brothers. Not wanting to pry, I nodded, lowering myself to sit by the fire on one of several logs they'd pulled up around it.

"He's curious," the older brother said.

"Might as well tell him," the younger replied.

With a sigh, the older brother turned my way, leaned forward, and said, "Never, and I mean never, try to fuck Rapunzel."

"Stop it," Elisa said with a laugh.

"I still blame her for it!" her brother said, his face only betraying the smallest hint of a smile. "You think she has a lot of hair upstairs? Try downstairs! I was trying to work my way into her entrance, but man—"

"That's when the attack came, catching us off guard," the middle brother said.

"All of you?" I asked.

He leaned back, grimaced, and shrugged.

"We were kinda… tag teaming her," the older brother said.

"To be fair, it was more of an orgy," the younger brother cut back in. "I still remember the way Prince Charming was watching as one of the evil step-sisters and Cinderella were going down on me, while the other step-sister was fingering my bum. It was all sorts of fucked up."

"But you loved it," the older brother said, laughing.

"I'm so sorry about them," Elisa said, looking horrified.

"Ah, come now," her older brother said. "As if your friend here hasn't had his fair share of fun? You playing innocent now, sis?"

She blushed, turning to the fire. I refused to say anything on the matter.

The younger brother scoffed, then looked at me with skepticism. "You're treating her right, aren't you?"

"He's the perfect gentleman," Pucky said, joining

me with a hand on my shoulder. "Now, weren't you telling a story?"

The older brother grinned. "Ah, right. So there I was, finally through the forest that is Rapunzel's nether regions, when a ball of flames erupted just outside the window. Screams followed, and all of us ran out to fight... forgetting we were naked."

"We still took out a good twenty or so of the witches before they had us."

"The witches?" I asked.

The oldest nodded. "Hekate wasn't among them. I hear she's on your side now?"

I nodded.

"Well, good. These ones served her, so if we ever meet the lady, we might have words to exchange."

"Noted," I replied.

"And you?" Nivian asked, turning the conversation back my way. "You've been doing well out there?"

I glanced around, wondering where Sekhmet and her sister were, but remembered the question. "Actually, it's been more of a struggle than I thought. For one, my clothes are still wet from when a fight took me into the river."

Red perked up at that, looking at me with concern, but it was Pucky, still standing at my side who ran a hand down my shirt and started to pull at it.

"We need to dry you off, get you out of these wet clothes," she said.

I pulled back, covering my torso again. "Maybe… not right here?"

Nivian looked away as if that would be enough, but Arthur chuckled, pointing back toward the other side of the clearing. "We set up a couple of tents over there, figuring staying here instead of trudging back would make sense. We had them for longer excursions, though Sekhmet took one."

"Yes, I was wondering about her."

"She went to find answers," Red said. "We told her she'd be better off waiting, but she insisted. Said she'd be fine, being a goddess and all."

I frowned, then chuckled. While they were all basically either Myths or Legends, it was interesting the way some considered themselves above the rest, simply because of how humanity had labeled them at some point or another.

"Well, I imagine she'll be fine," I said, then started toward where Arthur had said the tents would be.

Red stood to join me, and then Pucky was there, too.

"You'll excuse me if I take the time to catch up with my brothers?" Elisa asked.

"Of course," I replied. "But... I don't really need help."

"What're you going to do, sit around naked by yourself?" Pucky asked with a grin.

"I figured you could at least use a red cloak while your clothes dried," Red added.

She had a point, though imagining myself walking around naked except for the cloak of Little Red Riding hood made me feel weird on all sorts of levels. I nodded, but more because the idea of their warmth was rather welcome right then.

We left the clearing and found Sharon there, standing watch. She'd caught our scent and was watching our arrival.

"Everything okay?" she asked.

"Don't worry, I'll relieve you in a few minutes," Red said with a wink.

"That's all you need?" I asked.

She laughed. "Presumptuous, much?" Her eyes roamed over me, then she nodded. "But yes, that should do it."

Pucky chuckled, and I knew exactly where this was going. The fact that they were going to give Sharon a turn, though, was interesting. First, I was looking forward to what I was getting comfortable with. The ladies led me into the tent, Pucky quick to strip off my clothes and then pull her own top off, pressing her breasts against me as she pressed her lips to my neck, hands caressing my back.

"Just trying to help you get warm," she said, seductively.

I laughed. "All the blood's going to one spot though. Will that still work?"

Red pressed up against me from behind, apparently nude now too, I realized as I felt her perky nipples, her soft breasts on my back. One of her hands found my almost-hard cock, held it as it stiffened the rest of the way, and then moaned.

"Mmmm," Red said, "it's on fire."

Pucky and Red were both pressed against me then, caressing my body as I ran my hands over them in turn. I loved the feel of their curves, appreciating the dip of Pucky's lower back one minute, grabbing a handful of Red's ass the next, and enjoying the celebration of flesh for what it was. Then we were kissing, tongues mixed between the three of us, my hands caressing breasts before moving south. I felt between their legs, curious who was wetter and making a little contest out of it in my mind. Finding Red to be the wetter of the two, I turned to Pucky and knelt, kissing along the way, then lifted her up to bring her to the ground so I could use my tongue and help out. Soon she was moaning and clutching me, Red's breasts against my back as she whispered into my ear that it was her turn.

I happily obliged, turning to go down on her while Pucky stuck her head between my legs to give me a blowjob from below. Red's pussy welcomed me, clit hard and easy to find, and soon I had her moaning as well.

When it was done, Pucky rolled me over, holding my cock with both hands and kissing the tip, but then pulled back.

"No…" I moaned, not wanting her to stop.

"You and Sharon," she said, and shrugged playfully. "We need to make sure you're not totally spent."

Red laughed at that, still lying on her back. "Take it from me. After that much pleasure, you don't want to move."

I nodded, but felt like I would explode.

"You look…." Pucky's eyes roamed over me, hungrily. "Changed."

"Not the same guy you met at the convention center, huh?" I asked.

Red laughed. "Not at all."

"Hey."

"Same person here," Pucky said, finger at my temple, then hand to my heart. "And here…" it lowered, grabbing my cock. "Though here? I'd say it's a bit used now."

"Time for a new one?" I asked, then laughed as I tried to cover any insecurity that might have crept into my voice.

Her eyes went wide, and she shook her head. "Never."

"Never?" I looked to Red, then, and she was considering me, eyes on my cock in Pucky's hand, then did something unexpected. She leaned in, kissed my cheek, and said, "Never."

It just didn't seem like something Red would've done or said. All of this was amazing and I would never do anything to jeopardize it, but I'd never even stopped to think about what it all meant.

Were all of these ladies feeling this way? Did they plan on being with me forever, as in like, marriage? I was pretty sure the standard idea of marriage to multiple people wasn't legal, but maybe in worlds like this it meant something else entirely.

I decided there was no better way to understand than to ask.

"When you say, 'forever,' what exactly do you mean?"

"Forever," Red frowned, as if that was all that needed saying.

"Right, yes. Good." I pursed my lips. "As in,

neither of you plans on ever leaving me? Ever… I don't know, messing around with another man?"

Both stared at me in shock.

"Would you… want us to?" Red asked, looking appalled.

"No!"

"Oh, good." Pucky chuckled. "For a minute there I thought you were going to say you wanted your old pal Chris thrown into the mix or something, and sorry, but—"

"I meant, leaving me, going and fucking someone else," I clarified.

"Why would you think that?" Pucky asked, and Red just sighed, looking at me with confusion.

"I'm not saying I thought that. I'm saying… I mean, where I come from, people date for a bit, fool around, maybe move in together and then decide if they want to get married. Usually. And if that happens, they're together forever."

"Are you asking if we want to marry you?" Red asked, skeptically. "Because I gotta say, this is a weird proposal if s—"

"No! I mean, not that I'd be opposed to it, if it even works that way with… I mean…"

"Jack. Calm down." Pucky finally released my cock, stroking my chest instead as she looked into my eyes. "What is it you're trying to say?"

"I don't know. I guess the idea of forever never crossed my mind. I hadn't really thought that far ahead."

"Forever might not be that long," Red pointed out.

The quickly increasing beat of my heart went into overdrive. "I don't need that reminder right now."

Pucky beeped my nose. Actually beeped it.

"What was that?" I asked.

"That was to get you to calm down, to stop taking everything so seriously all of a sudden." She laughed. "Hey, who in here just saw some titties?" She wiggled her breast in front of my face. "Eh?"

"You… you've seen Garden State?"

She grinned and nodded. "So… everyone calm down."

"It's not an exact quote," I pointed out, now eyes focused on her breasts. To my surprise and relief, they were actually calming me down. "But I'll take it."

Red started dressing, handing me her red cloak to cover up. "We said forever, and that scared you. Well, here's how it is—you're the protector. You will be until you die. And we're with you—so, what? You think you'll want to 'date' other girls?"

"I…" Of course not, but I felt like I was walking into a trap and froze.

She pulled the cloak back, slightly. "You want other girls, after all of this?"

"No. Definitely not."

"So, then…?"

I took the robe, sitting up and wrapping it around me. "I'd just never thought about it before. Yeah. Yes. I do."

"What?" they both said at once.

"I mean, I want to be with you all forever," I explained, having never been such a bumbling idiot as far back as I could remember. "What you've given me, the fact that each of you by yourselves is amazing, and as a whole… I mean, it's more than I could ever hope so."

"Forever?" Pucky asked, head tilted.

I nodded. "Forever."

We might not have known each other long, but in the short amount of time I'd been with these ladies, we'd gone through more than most people would in a lifetime. Sure, Red could be a bit standoffish or emo at times, Pucky a bit clingy, Elisa a bit… posh? And now there was Sharon in the mix, and I didn't even know what to make of Sekhmet and Bastet. There was excitement, and areas for us to work on.

But looking at my life going forward, I couldn't possibly imagine it any other way than with them.

"I'll get Sharon, see if she wants to come in," Red said, turning for the tent flaps.

"Red," I whispered.

She turned, back, one eyebrow arched. I went to her, took her hands, and kissed her. Just a gentle caress of the lips at first, but then she was reciprocating, and we were kissing passionately. She even pushed me up against the 'wall,' forgetting we were in a tent, and we almost fell over.

Pucky was there to stabilize us, and as we were pulling apart I thought I heard Red whisper something.

"What was that?" I asked.

She opened her mouth, said, "I lo…" But then blushed, glancing down at my once again exposed cock. Up and ready to go. "I'll let her know you're ready."

As she stepped out, grabbing my clothes to hang by the fire, I turned to Pucky and asked, "What was that?"

"All this talk," Pucky said with a shrug. "Probably got her thinking, connecting with some emotional, caring side she tries to hide too often."

I nodded, completely understanding that feeling

at the moment. My emotions were swelling about as much as the blood to my crotch.

Red moved close to me, waving her hips as if about to rub herself on my leg. "I can be playful, fun. Caring."

A surge of desire ran through me.

"Don't leave me like this," I said, reaching for her hand, trying to put it back on my cock.

Red slapped my wrist, playfully. "Nu-uh, big guy. You need to have something left over for the new girl."

The idea of Sharon bringing me to orgasm? Okay, no complaints there.

Pucky, for her part, grinned, ran a hand up my chest, and then gave me a little slap. Light, playful. "You treat her nicely, okay? If I hear you were too rough with her…"

"You'll punish me?"

She laughed. "I'll be mad you weren't so rough with me."

"Oh, shit." She smiled, bent over to put on her pants in a way that gave me a perfect view of her ass and pussy, then looked over, laughed, and stood to pull the pants on the rest of the way. "Enjoy."

She was out, still putting on her shirt.

Red wrapped her robe around me and licked my ear. I pulled away because it tickled, and she grinned.

"Gotta keep you warm," she said, referring to the robe. "Plus, you'll want to give her a present to open."

I grabbed her by the waist, pulling her in for a quick kiss. Her tongue was warm, soft.

"Seriously, I don't know how you keep it up this long."

"If you were with you, you'd understand."

Her head tilted, she scrunched her nose, then nodded. "Confusing, but yes. Okay. I have an ever-lasting clit boner for you too."

With that weird imagery, she left me alone in the tent, cloak wrapped over my shoulders, waiting on Sharon.

7

There was a rustling and Sharon poked her head in. "Oh, you're…" Her eyes were on me, nude and exposed.

I pulled the robe around myself. "Sorry for that."

Her eyes rose to meet mine, her lip curling up.

"What?" I asked.

"Remember… remember how we first met?"

I laughed. "How could I not?"

Instantly, her cheeks were red, her eyes cast down. "I… I'm sorry."

"No, come on." I scooted closer, a hand on hers. "Don't be like that. You've changed. I've changed. We… we're together now."

Her eyes rose to meet mine again. "Specifically, I was talking about the staircase. How… maybe, I would've liked to finish that."

"Oh." My eyes went wide as blood rushed south. There was no doubt in my mind what she was referring to, especially when she suddenly switched gears, pushing me back playfully, then reaching behind me, moving the robe aside so I was exposed, and pausing.

"Say the word," she said, finger ever so gently running along my hip, closer and closer.

"Yes," I said. "I want it."

"That's not the word."

"Um… am I supposed to howl or something?"

She twitched at that, hand gripping my cock, hard. Honestly, she could've just done that and I'd have been satisfied for the night.

"Shit, sorry, I didn't mean anything by it." I squirmed, glad to see the crazy leaving her eyes as her grip loosened. Oddly, the moment had turned me on even more.

"What did you say that day, do you remember?" she asked.

"Err." I racked my brain, and then, miraculously, it came back. "It wasn't me!"

She smiled wide, moved aside to watch as she did it, and then pulled out my cock. "You're exactly who I'm looking for," she said, voice seductive, almost a purr. The words she'd said to me that day, too, though in a very different manner. Eyes focused on my cock, still, she started stroking it, gripping it tight, moving her hand along my shaft and then running her thumb along the head, as if studying what would happen.

"I love your cock," she said. "See the way it—"

"Don't need the details," I said with a nervous chuckle, really not sure I wanted to have my cock's intricacies explained to me.

"Less talk, more of…" She lowered herself, eyes on mine now, as she licked the tip playfully. "More of that?"

I breathed deep, nodded, and then watched with fascination as she kissed it, ran her tongue back down to my balls, and then circled it before taking the whole thing in her mouth. A squirm took hold, conveying a feeling I'd been trying to keep hidden. As much as I adored her, and wanted her, she was still the Big Bad Wolf, still the girl who'd tried to kill me more than once. The one plagued by darkness, though she was mastering it quite well. The idea of having my nut in her mouth was both exciting… and terrifying.

She saw this in my expression, pulled back, and pouted. But only briefly. "We can use this to our advantage."

"What's that?" I glanced down, both of us clothed now except for my erect cock hanging out.

"This… unease," she went on. "We can use it, I think."

"Go on."

She stood, slowly undressing until she was over me, completely nude. I shouldn't have expected the Big Bad Wolf to be shaven downstairs, but I was a bit surprised to see that she wasn't even trimmed. With her wild hair above, it actually worked, in that animal instinct sort of way.

"Wolf style," she said, and then turned around, sticking out her ass.

"Excuse me?"

"Just, like doggy, but I want you to get into it. Whenever you have a negative thought, fuck it away."

"I'm not going to—"

"Shut up and fuck me."

That wasn't something most guys need to be told twice, so I pushed myself up, removing the robe, and figured I'd give it a go. My cock rubbed along her ass, then slid into the folds of her pussy, feeling how wet she was for me. At first I went slow, loving the arch of her back, the clench of her pussy, the shape of her ass and the feel of it when I squeezed.

She shifted her hips and started getting into it, moving up and down on my cock, until I couldn't take it anymore and was clenching her hips, thrusting with a slapping sound as my hips hit her ass. And sure enough, when a shadow started to come over me, I growled, going harder, faster, and each time it was like we'd leveled up in the fuck zone.

She came first, and then twisted around and rode me a few minutes before climbing off and finishing me off with her hands, so that my cum shot out over the ground beside her. She eyed it, smiled, and then turned back my way.

"I wanted you to… you know, inside… But—"

"No, yeah. Of course."

She giggled. "And you're… feeling better?" She propped up on her side and my eyes went to her tits, and she cleared her throat, grinning. "Up here, perv."

I laughed, giving her a kiss. "Much."

And it was true. Unleashing like that, it made me look at her in a different light. While before I'd thought of her as part of the team, sure, there still hadn't been a full connection, a full level of trust we had desperately needed if we were going to charge back to Earth to fight the gods.

But now, with this? I could be charging into the pits of hell itself and be certain the flames wouldn't touch me. Her large, brown eyes staring into mine, it was almost easy to forget who she had once been, or rather, who she still was. This woman wasn't some delicate flower, some innocent little girl—in spite of her small frame, the way her eyes took me in like I was the only one to ever be there for her like this.

No, she was the Big Bad Wolf. And in its own, weird way, that turned me on.

Her eyes showed hesitancy, and she looked away.

"What?" I asked.

"You look at me… in a way that I don't deserve to be looked at."

I took her cheek in my hand, stared into her eyes, and said, "Never believe that. You deserve the best, and I plan on giving it to you."

She grinned, laughed. "I thought you just did?"

"That's not what I meant."

"I know."

She placed her hand on mine, pulled it down, staring at my palm as she traced it with one of her fingers. "My life hasn't been all sunshine and rainbows."

"I'm well aware."

She looked up at me. "And are you aware of the pain I've caused in others? The suffering because—"

I put a finger to her lips. "That wasn't you."

Her eyes glinted in the faint light, her lower lip trembling, and she nodded. "Still…"

"Tell me," I said.

Her mouth fell open, eyes looking horrified. "No."

"I once stepped on a snail. Broke its shell and felt horrible." I took her hand, squeezing it. "Now your turn."

She chuckled, but shook her head. "No, I'm not playing that game. But… but you should know, I ran with a pack for a while."

"Other werewolves?"

She laughed. "I'm not exactly a werewolf. I'm something more… but yeah. They looked up to me, and sure, I was under the influence of the shadow, but at times I have to admit, it wasn't like I was fighting to break free. Fighting to say forget that, to go good."

I nodded, knowing she was opening up, and that there wasn't anything I could say that would make her past go away.

"We were tearing up this neighborhood, trying to teach them a lesson." She breathed deep, eyes distant as she remembered it. "Then we get to this one house, almost a shack, really. And I'd just torn off the door, when I turned to see this little boy there, staring at me with wide eyes. Then his mom runs up, grabbing him, holding him tight… whimpering. She actually whimpered at the sight of me, frightened for the life of her little boy."

"You… didn't?"

She shook her head, to my relief. "I was their leader, or so I thought. When I refused to hurt that family? They all turned on me. The family got away, but I paid for it… took a beating that, if I couldn't self-heal, would've likely left me dead."

"That's… horrible."

"Now, here with you?" She hesitated, breathed, and then spoke real fast. "I don't ever feel like I'll have to worry about that again."

I pulled her close and kissed her cheek. "You're one of us. We won't ever let anyone hurt you. Ever."

"Nor I you," she replied, letting an elongated fingernail grow into a claw that she ran down my leg, just enough for me to feel it without it actually hurting. A reminder that she was powerful in her own right.

"I wasn't always perfect you know."

She eyed me, then shook her head. "Yes, you were. Compared to what I've been, you've always been a perfect angel."

Truth.

I kissed her, feeling the way her lips were rougher than Red's, but in a way that made me feel an excitement for life, a sense of adventure. That kiss sent images through my mind of running through fields with her, chasing down prey and devouring it raw.

When she looked at me again, her eyes showed passion and affection. She stood, reaching for her clothes, and said, "Let's go, join the others. It's time we figured out what our next steps should be in this fight."

We returned to the fire to find Elisa and her brothers were gone, I imagined walking the perimeter, catching up while also keeping watch. Nivian had her arms around Arthur's waist, though he still glowed a light blue and looked like she'd slip right through him. He kissed her on the forehead and said, "Someday, my dear," in a way that made me feel like I'd walked in on something.

I nudged Sharon and took a step back. Arthur must have sensed me though, because his head moved slightly, but he didn't say anything.

I kept going, guiding Sharon back.

"What was that about?" Sharon asked when we stopped a few paces off.

"They seemed… seemed like they could use some alone time."

She nodded, then looked at me. "You're shivering?"

"Am I?" I truly hadn't noticed.

"Come on." She moved the red robe aside, eyes

on mine, and moved in, then made me wrap the robe around both of us. It was like we were wrapped up in a large blanket, me completely nude in there, she less so, her hands roaming over me, moving to create friction.

I moaned, whispering, "Damn, that feels good."

"Better?" she asked.

With a nod, I held her tight, slipping my hands into the back of her pants to grab her ass. She laughed, shaking it slightly for emphasis. For the longest time, we stood there, her head on my shoulder, our hands appreciating each other's bodies. Finally, Arthur appeared, nodded, and motioned that we could go away if we wanted.

"Oh, no," Sharon said, seeing this. She helped me keep the robe closed as she stepped away, grinning and motioning me to go on. "You two talk if you need to, I've taken more than my fair share of Jack, here. already."

Arthur chuckled, surely getting the joke. "Thanks, Sharon. We'll be along shortly."

"Nivian?" I asked.

"The others returned," Arthur explained. "She's in good company."

Arthur watched Sharon go, then turned to me. I was struck by his regal posture, the look of confidence in his eyes I wondered if I'd ever project like that.

"You're a lucky man, you know that?" he said.

I laughed. "More than I deserve, for sure."

"Don't sell yourself short. What you're putting yourself through, the risks and all that. While you could make a point that nobody deserves so many beautiful, amazing women—if anyone does, I'd say it's you." Before I could argue, he held up a hand. "And I'm not only saying that based on what you've done in the past, but what you'll do in the future. You're going to really have to push yourself going forward, but I see something in you, a burning fire behind those eyes. As long as you stay true, we have no worries."

Taking a moment to process this, I nodded, then said, "Thank you."

He nodded, gesturing me to walk, and we started off together. "All that said, it's a good a time as any to tell you."

"Yes?"

"Weird things are afoot," Arthur said. "Sekhmet sent a message through Nivian, a vision of sorts, of what I can only describe as energy leaving this world, when it shouldn't. Keep an eye open, and be wary."

"I will," I promised. It took me a moment, but I

decided being open with him was necessary. "There was someone out there…"

"Someone?"

"A fairy. A queen."

"The fairy queen, you mean?" Arthur considered this, then shook his head. "Impossible."

"What do you mean?"

"I mean, she was banished from this world. Exiled. I don't… no, there's no way it was her. Find out more, would you?"

I nodded, following him.

"You know," he guided me to an incline, which we ascended until we reached a point that allowed us to see over the trees to the south, "There was a time in life that, if I'd just turned away, not taken the leap, all of this could have turned out very differently."

"How so?"

He stared out at the now dark sky, eyes piercing it as if seeing something beyond my ability to see. "I took the sword."

"Excalibur?" I asked.

"That's right. The sword that Merlin had cursed, knowing I was destined to be the one. The sword that turned me into what I became, that cursed me and my men to a life of the night."

"But not anymore."

"Not anymore." He offered me a smile, then clasped my shoulder. "You're making us all proud, my boy. Keep it up, and we'll see victory."

Warmth filled my chest, pride and a sense of duty. I wasn't doing this for the pride of King Arthur, that was for sure. But it did help.

"I won't' let you down," I replied, and we stood there like that, staring out at the night in silence, simply enjoying the moment.

8

As the sun rose over the Fae world, Arthur already had me up and heading back into the mists.

"You've grown strong, but it isn't strong enough," he insisted. "Keep at it, and as you gain prana, try thinking outside the box."

"What's that supposed to mean?" I asked.

He gave me a knowing smile. "I believe in you."

I frowned at his cryptic answer, but stood tall at the thought that the legendary Arthur was giving me advice at all. That would never get old.

Soon I was back in the mists, my clothes no longer damp, but my mood... not so optimistic. While I loved leveling up and getting stronger and knew it was important for the fight to come, one day in the mists had been more than enough. At least, enough for my patience.

Even so, I didn't balk at my duty. If killing Shades was what it would take to grind, to get to that next level and be ready to fight, so be it. Plus, Arthur and the ladies had pumped me up.

Gathering my bearing in the mists was tough, but I did my best to head back in the direction I'd seen the fairy. Too bad the sword didn't lead me in reverse. Stumbling along, trying to see, I found something else strange—dark shapes like Shades, only they would move away from me whenever I got close, and at one spot I swear I'd seen a ripple of light and then the Shades vanished.

It was entirely possible I had only imagined it happening, but they definitely seemed to be vanishing, not just running away. By mid-morning I was getting irritated, and by mid-day, bored. So it was that, when I finally came to a ledge and looked down at a group of Shades moving along below like a river of black, I didn't wait to assess the situation. Sword held up with both hands, I leaped down upon them.

Old me wouldn't have done that. Hell, me from even a few days ago probably wouldn't have done it. But at this point I was looking for something to kill, and was just glad it happened to be Shades. A few of them noticed me and swung up, but their attacks didn't reach me, I was too fast. Landing with a burst outward that pushed back the closest ones and sent a group attack through the first wave, I was up and slashing a moment later.

Prana floated over as I charged again, starting to get smart and putting the cliff face to my back, to prevent them from surrounding me. I blocked and my energy shield popped up, then I dismissed it and went back in at them with wild strikes, my Tempest tattoos glowing, pulling in the mists, giving me strength.

As I was fighting though, I started to realize what a badass I'd become. The idea that I needed a wall was silly, and in fact I wanted more around me so that when I cut down one group, another would be waiting behind me to get killed.

So I jumped and, to my surprise, found that my tempest ability when charged like that allowed me almost to run on the mists! It was crazy, using it like I had in games with a double jump. I could leap up, push off of the mists—as long as there was mist to push off from—and then redirect my trajectory. With that new understanding of my powers, I was able to move about this group quickly. Soon I had taken down all in my vicinity, and moved for more in the direction they were going.

Three of them appeared, larger than the rest, but

with a few swings of my sword two were without heads, the third cut in half at the torso. He soon had his head in half as well, and I moved on.

Suddenly I froze.

Past them, in the direction the horde had been going, was what I could only assume was a portal. Clear as ever one moment, barely visible by the mists the next. It was black, rippling, like oil on the ocean, but vertical.

"What's this...?" I started, looking around for answers. All I found was death and some straggling green balls of light moving into me.

Moving toward the portal, running now as it started to fade, I noticed something—a face, turning to look my way, eyes piercing, and then... it was gone.

Those eyes were familiar, but from where?

Now that the portal was gone, along with the Shade horde, I turned, first thinking it would be a good time to upgrade. Then again, with all this prana in me and remembering how being a Tempest meant I should be able to manipulate the mists, I decided to try an experiment. Arthur had said to think outside the box, so I focused on my inner self as he'd said, but tried seeing if there was a way to use the prana, instead of upgrading my stats, to increase my Tempest power. More than skills, I meant to physically shift the mists, move them out of my way, to be able to see what was going on.

I dug deep, imagining the flowing green energy and envisioning it as part of me. As my skin tingled and a warmth expanded in my chest, I saw myself as one with the prana, using it to affect my surroundings. When I opened my eyes, the sight caused me to catch my breath.

The mists were actually moving! Swirling out, sweeping past me in way that was so unnatural, it could have only been caused by an outside force.

A shape appeared, darkness in the mist with large, flapping wings, and it was almost upon me! I dove aside as the beast emerged from the mist. A massive lion, larger than the largest two I'd ever seen put together, with wings spread out.

And then it was gone again, into the mists.

I stared, confused. It wasn't I that had caused the mists to move, but that winged lion. Frowning, sword out and at the ready in case it returned and attacked me, I prepared again, trying to focus on my core, on doing the unthinkable.

A roar, and the mists flew out from around me, that lion there, standing, wings folded. It closed its mouth and stared at me.

One hand out, other on the sword that I lowered

just in case, I tried to look as nonthreatening as possible.

"Whoa there," I said, no other words coming to mind.

It lingered, watching. The mists returned, moving between us, and then it was gone. At first I wasn't sure whether to feel relief or some other emotion at the lion being gone, but figured I'd give the strange prana usage a break, for now. Instead, I increased my stats again, bringing my strength to three-hundred percent, my speed to two-hundred and ten, and threw some at my shield and other skills, giving them extra boosts in how powerful they were and how long they would last.

That night when I returned, as exhausted as I was, it didn't matter. As Arthur pointed out, we weren't here only for my training against the Shades and my upgrades, but to work on all aspects of my abilities. He cleared a circle and had me practice with Red for some swordplay.

Going up against Red was an entirely different experience than the Shades. For one, I couldn't rely on my other skills so much, because then I knew she'd do the same. Her, with that cloak of hers? No thanks.

Then there was the fact that she was a genuine badass. Mrs. Little Red Riding Hood herself, who'd

gone up against none other than the Big Bad Wolf—
often times a different version of said wolf than the
one leaning against a tree and watching us right
now. She was the latest, though, and from what I'd
recently learned, the first female. Good thing for me!

Red knew she was badass, and loved it. When I
came at her and she flipped me onto my back,
quickly straddling me and sticking her knife at my
throat, her eyes betrayed the fact that she rarely had
as much fun as in these moments.

"Hot," I said, and she moved her hips against me
slightly before getting up.

"Don't rely on your size, especially not the size of
your sword," she winked, and I wasn't sure how to
take that. Had she just made a jibe at the size of my
dick? Surely not.

Deciding to take it as playful instead of going the
insecure man route, I laughed, and charged again.
Only, this time I made an effort of taking her advice,
faking right and going for a kick instead of
the sword.

"Better," she said, moving out of the way of the
kick and swiping my leg aside. "Now don't
get cocky."

"Dammit," I grunted as she managed to get
behind me, standing this time but still, blade to my
throat.

"And don't get frustrated," Pucky shouted from the sidelines.

"You've seen how much I've been training," I countered, annoyed that I was sounding annoyed, "I've been upgrading speed and strength like crazy, and still she gets me."

"A few days," Red said, scoffing, "compared to a lifetime?"

"But I'm supposed to be this grand protector, this—"

I lunged, catching her off guard, and pinning her to the ground with a quick kiss. She shoved me off, at first mad, then laughing.

"You scoundrel."

"Hey," I stood back, sword ready, "taking advantage of the moment."

"Whatever it takes," Elisa said, nodding in approval.

"Try to get my sympathy again, see what happens," Red said, brushing off her cloak.

"Lucky me, I don't need sympathy." I charged again, this time hoping that she'd think I would try a trick, and it worked. She dodged where she thought I'd fake strike and come in at, but instead I went straight for her, so that her cloak whipped in the wind and pulled her out of harm's way.

Next, I spun fast and grabbed her by the waist—

only to be flipped over and put in an arm bar, both of our weapons flying to the dirt nearby.

"Well, it was a good effort," she admitted, helping me up.

Arthur was talking to Nivian and said he had to go, but directed us to keep training. Red took some time to show me more moves, some new blocks based on how fast and strong I was becoming.

By the time Arthur returned, we were breaking for food and water.

"Heard from Sekhmet?" I asked.

"Actually, yes." He gathered us all around. "She's reported seeing what should have been large communities, empty. Thinks they're making a move on Earth."

"That checks with what I've been seeing in the mists," I said. "Portals, I think."

He shook his head. "This doesn't bode well for our return, but…" His eyes focused on me, intently. "Portals? And you saw some sort of fairy queen, you said?"

"That's right."

He ran a hand along his jaw, then frowned. "It's possible…"

"She's bringing them through?" Elisa offered.

"That's what I was starting to wonder about, yes."

"So we all go into the mists, seek her out," Red offered. "Put a stop to this."

"I think the fact that she's shown herself to Jack means something," Arthur replied. "He'll go back again, tomorrow. But this time—really focus. You're not going out there just to train, though you should get every opportunity you can. Your goal is to find her. Got it?"

I nodded.

He patted me on the back, indicated Sharon, and said, "Work with her on the Shadows, making sure you can keep it at bay when challenged, and then get some sleep. Back at it tomorrow and then… We've been experimenting with the lake and Nivian's powers, making progress, and I think it's almost time you all made a return to Earth."

9

The rest of them went off to gather more food and put together a fire, while Sharon waited for me, her arms wrapped defensively around her body.

Her smile faltered when I approached, replaced by a look of apprehension.

"That bad?" I asked.

"What?"

"I don't know, my stink or something?" I chuckled. "You got this super nervous look in your eyes as I came toward you just now.

"No, it's just…" She glanced around, nodded for me to follow her, and we walked off a little way into the woods. Stopping there, she took my hand, eyeing it apprehensively. "Shadows… you know. I've only really started to master this myself, and now I'm supposed to show you."

"Good point." When her eyes met mine, I added, "But I believe in you."

"Yeah?"

"I'm putting myself in your hands, Sharon."

She smiled, gave my hand a squeeze, and then said, "In that case, try to keep up."

"What do you mean?" I asked, but she was already running.

I chased after her, jogging at first, then sprinting, wanting to ask her how she expected this to go. She knew I'd been leveling up, that her speed couldn't match mine, unless… The realization hit me at the same time as she started to transform, first just wolf ears and claws, a tail, and then she was lurching forward, going full wolf on me.

And when I say wolf, I mean a *huge* wolf. Her eyes met mine and she growled, then pushed on, at least twice as fast as I could go at my top speed.

"There's no way…" I started, and then blinked. Did she want me to actually become the wolf, too? Granted, there was still some of that left in me, but the only time I'd let it out, it had taken complete control. Then again, doing so made sense considering what she was trying to teach me. If I still had it, control was necessary.

Dammit.

I pushed on, reaching deep within, trying to find that wolf in there. It was no good, but it wasn't like that was a surprise. More was needed to reach that point. Not just more focus, but a darker focus.

Remembering what it had been like to be out there killing Shades, focusing on the anger that had taken over when I'd seen Red and the others in harm's way before, and letting the rage boil over, I felt it coming.

Trembling at first, everything around me darkening as if the shadows were reaching out for me. Then they were on me, taking hold, and I was growing, transforming, taking on the form of a wolf. Nothing like her as far as size goes, but nothing to laugh at either. And maybe she was going slower than normal, or maybe it was my upgrades, but I was catching up.

She sniffed the air and turned to see me running up at her side, welcoming me with a howl, and then we were in the hills, running like nothing else in this world or ours mattered. Two wolves, owning the night, the wind coursing through our fur, the ground flying past underneath our paws.

A growl caught me off guard and she lunged at me, but I pulled back, out of the way, and stared, confused. She was circling me, teeth bared, eyes ferocious. My shadow started to deepen, my desire to tear her limb from limb sending an acidic saliva dripping down my chin.

Only here, eyes didn't show shadow, they didn't show a red glow or anything like that. This was her, testing me.

With that in mind, I was able to focus on her, to remember the way she'd squeezed my hand before running off… and the shadow faded. Seeing her like that, now, still circling me, putting on a show, ignited another part of my wolf form that I hadn't even considered. Having a wolf boner was a strange sensation, in part because it was about four times what I was used to, and also because it was dangling out for all the world to see.

She noticed—how could she not? And paused. Was that a smile?

With a nod toward the hills, she took off in a trot, starting to change back as we reached a cave. Our clothes were gone, lost somewhere along the way, likely torn. Maybe we'd find them on the way back. Hopefully repairable. But we didn't care. I was following her into a dark cave, my eyes still not fully transformed so that I could better see where I was going.

With a snicker, she disappeared through a corridor, but her laugh was cut off. I ran, worried something had happened to her. She was standing there, eyes full of wonder as she took in what I then saw was an underground network of pools of water.

They were turquoise, a white and blue glow coming from the center of each, tiny speckles of light rising up like bright dust on a lazy sunny afternoon.

"Spiritual pools," she said, and began working her way down the slope toward them.

I stood there, watching her bare back, her beautiful ass. She almost slipped, and I darted forward to catch her. She smiled up at me, licked her lips at my nudity, and then we helped each other the rest of the way down.

Finally, Sharon led me to one of the spiritual pools of water, where she dipped herself in, and reached down to scrub. I started moving to join in, but she held up a hand, shooed me back, and then got out.

"What..." I started, but realized what was going on when she got down on all fours, ass facing me, face just above the water.

She didn't have to say it, and this time, I was ready. I fucking loved her, just like I loved all of them. There wasn't a thing I could think of I wouldn't do if any of them asked. Okay, maybe a couple things, but this... Her cute little pink butthole was there just above her pussy, both calling to me. I knelt, looking around her to see that she was staring at her reflection in the water, and I had to ask.

"What's up with—"

"I've always been curious what I would look like while you did this, so... that's all. Call it an experiment."

I hesitated, then went back to my business. Kneeling, I took my cock and slid it up her thigh, along her pussy, about to slide in, when she reached back, a hand in the way.

"How's the saying go?" She glanced over, bit her lip. "You've got to lick it, before you...?"

"Oh, sure, of course."

I got down, unsure what the best position was, going for her pussy from behind, but she said, "Um... Not there."

"Sorry?" I sat back up, hands moving up her thighs. She didn't look back, so I assumed she was embarrassed, maybe? Then it hit me why. She didn't want me to lick her pussy, she wanted me to lick what was currently above her pussy. Her cute little asshole.

She had just washed it, thoroughly, I supposed. I'd never done that, and the idea made me squirm. Then again, this was Sharon. There wasn't much I wouldn't do for anyone on the team, so I repositioned myself, kissing her ass cheek, hand moving down between her legs, caressing her clit as my lips and tongue made their way to the center of her ass. She was squirming, clearly loving it, and when my tongue flicked the edge of her asshole, she let out a short gasp. Then a low moan.

Damn, if it was going to give her that much pleasure, I was going all in. But first… a little tease. I moved around it, tongue darting out, lips kissing her closer, then a bit away. One more tongue along her pussy, and then was up on her ass, kissing it, licking it, doing whatever I could without having a clue what I was supposed to do.

Her moans were reward enough, but when she finally pushed herself back and grabbed my cock, nuzzling her face in it and growling, I knew this was going to be fun. She took it deep in her mouth, hand massaging my balls, and then she looked at me with mischievous eyes.

"Now, Shadow training," she said, and started to transform. "If you lose yourself, focus on our connection. On me and you, not just physical, but emotional."

"But—"

Her finger, a long claw on it now, went to my mouth. "Ravage me."

My cyes went wide, and before I knew it my

instincts took over, the animal in me unleashing. We were both wolves, but it was like I wasn't there at all, as I was on her, taking her from behind. The pleasure was intense, my ultra large wolf cock sensing each thrust with many times the pleasure spots than I was used to.

Sure, getting the position was awkward, but soon we had it and she was yelping away, reaching orgasm in wolf form. I got close too, railing away on her and even starting to nibble at her shoulders, but then focused… reeling myself back in.

As the last of her orgasm faded, we started our transformation back.

Flesh, skin on skin again, no wolf fur, no animal noises. Well, maybe some animal noises. She reached back, slid my cock out, and then shifted her hips down, sliding it into another hole. Holy shit, it was tight.

"Now you can cum," she whispered, bracing herself as I slowly slid the entire length of my cock into her ass.

It only took a few thrusts with how tight she was, how aroused I'd already been from everything we were doing up to that point. Pleasure took hold, not just from her ass but with all of the pleasure points from the experience before piling up, so that when my orgasm hit it was like she was there, pulling it out of me, until there was nothing left.

My cock throbbed in her ass, my body giving out so that I had to collapse onto her, one hand on the ground to steady myself, the other reaching around to massage her breasts. I breathed heavily, kissed her back, and then slowly pulled out.

She turned to me, folding her legs around like in a yoga stretch, and kissed me. "Now you're getting the hang of this shadow business."

I laughed. "That's all it took?"

"We'll work on it some more, I'm sure," she replied, causing a surge of aftershock from the orgasm to go through me.

I kissed her back, accepted her hand as she led me into the pool to bathe, and said, "I look forward to it."

10

Arthur had me training in this sort of pattern for days. Going out into the mists to fight Shades and get stronger, testing my abilities, returning to work on the other aspects of being a protector each night. He kept stressing that there had to be more out there, and that I needed to find this supposed queen of the fairies again, but so far neither was happening.

It got to the point that, although I'd never been stronger or so fulfilled, I was starting to doubt myself. Had I really seen the queen of fairies at all? Or even those large statues, which I hadn't seen again since that first day. And the lion? The rest of it?

On the morning of the fourth day, Pucky woke

me up extra early, hand caressing my cheek, and her warm smile was a comforting first sight.

"What's up?" I whispered.

She ran her hand down toward my crotch, then winked. "Just joking, I'm not that corny. Come on, I have something else in mind."

I glanced around at the others in the tent, still sleeping, so pushed myself up to follow her, trying to stay quiet. She led me out to one of the nearby trees, then stopped and turned to me, head tilted as she stared into my eyes.

"What's... up?" I chuckled. "For real, this time."

She grinned, and then I noticed her horns glowing. "Just wanted to check on you, see how you're doing with the training. It's not much, but hopefully enough."

"Is this another test?" I asked.

Her eyes moved across my face, as if reading me, then one hand went to my cheek, caressing it, moving through my hair. I started to lean forward to kiss her, but saw that wasn't what this was. Her hands traveled down through my hair and to my neck, as her eyes penetrated me. Then they were back to the front, on my chest, stopping over my heart.

"You're strong," she said. "And I don't mean just

physically, though obviously the last few days have been kind to you."

"In more ways than one," I said with a grin.

She chuckled, then took my hands, and placed one on her cheek. "Look. See."

I wasn't following, but figured doing what she'd been doing was my best bet, here. So, moving my hand along her cheek, feeling her soft, warm skin and enjoying the moment for what it was, I stared into her eyes, looking for whatever I was supposed to be seeing.

"Look deeper," she said, and moved my hand, up, so that as she dropped her hands back to my chest, I was caressing her temples, then her forehead. I paused, continuing to her horns. It's a strangely erotic feeling, touching a woman's horns. Every man knows the awkward feeling when they grab a cucumber or a banana and realize it must be similar to how a woman feels when she's grabbing your cock. Well, horns like hers were similar, in that they weren't bright blue or red or anything like that, but almost the same tone as her skin, and moving my hands along them I almost felt like I was stroking two cocks at once.

Yeah, like I said, weird… for a straight guy.

She bit her lip, enjoying the moment but also humored. "Focus."

I nodded, eyes roaming over her, seeing every bit of her, even the small freckles around her nose, the little mole at her hairline, just barely hidden, the glow that radiated off her horns. Then my hands were in her hair, and she was breathing heavily as they ran down to her neck, over her shoulders.

That moment could've easily led into many others like it, but I knew that wasn't the purpose of this exercise. Focusing, I ran my hands over to her heart, really trying to see, as she'd asked.

A glimmer formed, something there but not there, radiating out of her, then all along her skin. Suddenly, I was seeing her! Really seeing her, and I don't mean some other version of her physical presence or whatever, but her life was before me, moments as a young teenager running from trouble, first learning how to use her powers and teleport, to the extent that she did. Then there was her with her first crush, a boy who looked very much like Prince Charming, or maybe it was one of the other princes, but he wasn't giving her the time of day. Teenage Pucky crying, teenage Pucky in the gym punching the shit out of a punch bag until it burst, teenage Pucky with friends over the years. I recognized some of those friends from fairy tales, including Bo Peep, the Huntsman, and Little Miss Muffet—who happened to have spider eyes. Creepy.

"You're seeing me," she said, her voice carrying through his mind like a song.

"I am," he replied. "Are you sure you want to show me—"

Suddenly my mind cut to her in a dark room, hand down her panties, as that's all she was wearing, as she vigorously touched herself.

She laughed. "Relax, I'm only showing you what I want to show you. This…" The image changed just as younger-her reached climax, switching to her reclining with a cup of coffee, eyes closed as classical flute carried to me from somewhere… distant, in the memory I guessed, though I hadn't heard any sound with the other memories.

Her smile felt different. Warmer.

The way her fingers found mine, more sensual. With a nod, she said, "You're going places, Jack. I'm glad to be there with you."

"Me too," I replied, not really sure where to go with that, but knowing the moment didn't allow for any joking or silliness.

"Ready?" Arthur's voice said, and we turned to see him leaning up against a tree nearby, grinning.

I nodded.

Pucky gave me a kiss on the cheek and waved us off, then vanished back into the woods. I assumed to work on her own magic, or maybe just to think.

How strange that she'd shown me such normal parts of her life, when I was certain there was so much more weird stuff she'd been through. What had happened was still beyond me, but while walking with Arthur I could sense a purity to the air I hadn't noticed at first, even more than normal. With each step I was aware of my muscles, of the movement of the wind, and even of the magic flowing through me.

"Your team," Arthur said, watching me as we walked, "they're keepers."

I laughed. "That's the understatement of the year."

He nodded. "I don't know what I'd do without Nivian."

"And… when she goes back? I mean, I assume she is going back, right? Do you think there's anything to what Sekhmet is looking into?"

"I hope so."

He didn't say anything more on the subject, but looked around at the light mist at the top of the trees. I looked too, noticing some little lights bouncing around up there—either fire flies or fairies. Having grown up in the city, both seemed equally magical.

"The mists… they're expanding," he said. "Not insignificant, that."

"They're linked to something?"

A nod. "The more the darkness expands on Earth, the more the mists take over here. They're not bad, or evil, in themselves. But if they were to take over this world, well…"

"Yin and Yang," I said, getting it. "It's okay to have some darkness and some light, but all of one ruins the balance."

"Essentially, yes. Which is why it's important you finish your training so wc can make our move soon."

I stopped, the mists just ahead, and turned to him. "You knew this was more than just about leveling up, or increasing my stats, didn't you?"

"There's always more, Jack. We had a feeling you'd find something, and think you're on the right track. Today's the day."

With a final nod of understanding, I placed my hand on the hilt of my sword, and made my way into the mists. They didn't feel as wet or cold that day, even seeming to move out of my way as I progressed. For a long time, I focused on my breathing, on keeping the connection to that feeling of awareness that Pucky had left me with, and staying alert in case there was trouble.

Working through a valley that had some similarities to one I'd been in the day before, I made for the far end and was halfway across when I felt eyes on me. Nothing visible, but I kept my wits about me, eyes searching. A wave of mist moved ahead and I froze, but it was only a Shade stumbling along. It paused, turned toward me with the darkness floating around it, and then charged.

A side step and a thrust took care of it. Without issue.

Then the feeling of being watched was back, and I spun to see outstretched wings. The lion was there, at the top of the valley. It stared at me as I started working my way up toward it, mists blocking my vision before I'd even got half way. Just as I'd almost reached the top, I heard a roar and a screech, followed by more, as three Shades lunged for me. As I took care of the first one my eyes quickly noted that another dozen or so were on the ground, dead. The next shade hit me though, body lunging through the air so that it knocked me over and I fell, tumbling back down the hill.

Cursing as I tumbled, a rock nearly hitting my head, but I managed to catch hold of shrubbery three quarters of the way down and catch myself. The Shade had come to a stop a few paces ahead of me, at a crouch and was about to attack. My sword had fallen loose at its feet, but I used my Tempest ability to change the mists, have them swirl around him. Only a distraction, but it worked. He turned as if expecting the lion, instead only getting me charging from below, fist in his gut. Then I lunged for the sword, had it as he recovered, and sliced at his thigh. Contact. The shade collapsed to one leg, hissed, and then his neck gave way to my steel. My head spun, eyes scouring the mists for the others. Had they rolled down? Found footing above me, waiting to attack?

I cautiously made my way back up, only seeing sky through the mist above, nothing ahead. Pushing out with my powers, the mist gave way before me to reveal the answer to my question about the shades. Only, there were more than a few—there were at least twenty there, turning to me, black eyes boring into me.

They charged, catching me off guard. I refused to fall again, but at the detriment to my defense. Two got strikes in, others catching me, nearly taking me to the ground. For the first time in those mists, I started to worry as more piled on.

A flash of wings. The lion overhead.

It didn't attack, but seeing it inspired something in me. I managed to wiggle out, to strike with my group attack, to absorb energy and push it back out, attacking those in the vicinity and creating room for myself to fight more sturdily.

Another sweep over by the lion, this time clear as day, its roar emitting a golden blast. I cringed, ready for it to hit me, even throwing up my shield. Only to my surprise, when the light hit me my chest surged with pride and confidence, my vigor and moral replenished.

In a matter of minutes, I'd taken out the last of the Shades, but saw no more sign of the lion. The mist was gone from this section of the fields by then, so that I was able to take in the green grass, a stream running into a larger lake. I wanted to catch my breath, to think over the attack and what I'd done wrong. Kneeling on the bank, I scooped up water to drink, and pulled out some of the crackers and dried meat Arthur had given me.

"Jack be nimble, Jack be quick," a voice said, "Jack jump over here with your little dick."

"Little?" I said, focusing on the wrong details, as I stood up, looking for the voice's source.

Laughter. A bright glimmer on the water, and then she was there, dancing across the surface—only this time she was like a spirit of light, appearing as a nude woman prancing across the lake, eyeing me, growing larger as she approached.

"You've found yourself a spirit animal, I see."

At first I frowned, then noticed a shadow, a gush of wings, and turned to see the lion there, approaching. Mane of gold, fur a lighter gold, almost white. Wings folding back.

Is that's what is happening here?" I kept my eyes on the winged lion.

"Of course, you have to earn its loyalty, don't you?" The fairy danced over into my line of sight. "But for some reason, it hasn't outright abandoned you yet."

"I see that."

She smiled at me seductively. "Must have a strong reason, must see something in you, something special. I wonder what that could be?" Her long eyelashes batted my way, but then she turned, smile fading. "Ooh, chat later. You've got company."

More fucking Shades. Only, this time when I swung my sword and took out two, I turned to see the lion mauling three more before flying up and dashing at another. Holy hell, fighting with a spirit animal was going to be fun. We tore through the rest of them in no time.

Basking in the glory of my kill, I watched the glowing runes float up from my sword, checked over my stats, and assigned them. Or I started to, but when I applied the first to strength, I noticed a line I hadn't seen before, connecting me to the lion. One that faded slightly. I applied another point, and the line faded more.

Odd. This time, instead of using the points I focused on that line, focused on redirecting the points there, and then seeing the green start to flow, I concentrated all of my unused prana on that connection and the lion.

With a roar, the lion stood tall, shook its mane, and then charged me. I almost had a heart attack, but instead of attacking, it pounded up next to me, rubbing its face against mine. That big, bushy main was there, rubbing against me, and I felt stronger and more awake.

Had I just formed some sort of bond with it? Some sort of spirit animal connection, I imagined. My guess was that I could now use any future prana to upgrade my stats, or strengthen this bond, maybe even bond more, if needed.

Either way, this was amazing. It purred, turned, and then circled me before glowing blue and fading into me. That was a trip, but when it was gone, I looked down at my chest to see a tattoo that was in an outline shape of a winged lion.

He'd just become one with me, formed with my Tempest abilities so that I could call on him when the time was right.

Holding my hand to that spot, I closed my eyes and saw him there, looking at me, waiting to see if I needed him.

"Not yet," I said, and gave him a nod like a bow.

He returned it, and then I lowered my hand. This was intense.

"See, your spirit animal," the fairy said, appearing again, seemingly materializing from the mists right next to us, growing larger until she was the queen of fairies again.

"You…"

She gave me a regal bow, then to the lion. "Keep him close, and you can't go wrong."

She faded again, leaving me to say, "What the fuck? Why's she keep doing that?"

The lion just looked at me.

"Come on then," I said, and started walking, glad to see the lion following. After a bit though, we paused as something caught my eye. Looking up, it was at first a shift in the mists, nothing more. Swirling white, a bit of gray. Then more gray, and there was a shadow. Only, of what? It seemed to rise over fifty feet into the air, humanoid, lumbering past me at a distance.

The lion was there at my side, growling at the shadow.

Darting forward, very much aware that maybe this would be a creature I stood no chance against, I had to get a better look. Arthur would've told me if things like this existed in the mists. He'd told me about the Shades, and as explained, they weren't these massive colossus beasts, or titans, or whatever this was.

The lion took up a defensive position. But as soon as it noticed the tall being, it was gone.

One minute it was there and then darkness and swirling mists, and the large, lumbering form had disappeared again. All gone.

Something here didn't fit, and I was pretty sure it warranted me telling the others. With that in mind, I turned, sword out, and started making my way back. My spirit lion seemed to understand and in a flash, the line formed between us again and it absorbed into my tattoo, gone from sight.

11

My return to camp in the middle of the day seemed to have caught the others off guard. For one, nobody was gathered around waiting for me, which made sense but was confusing. I spotted Red and Pucky sparring, throwing some wicked punches and kicks, and heard moaning coming from one of the tents. Waiting for it to finish, I found it was what I assumed when Arthur stuck his head out and grimaced.

"Oh… Oh." He shrugged. "Sorry."

"Can you… I mean, as a spirit, or?" I asked.

Arthur chuckled, glancing back at Nivian. She was stepping around him, emerging from the tent as she dressed, not bashful in the slightest. "Not that it's

any of your business, but he can please me on a spiritual level that he never could when only a man."

"Meaning no," Arthur said. "Not in the
same ways."

"Oh, sorry." I'd only been joking around, not
thinking it was really an issue.

"Well," another voice from behind said, and I
spun around to see the queen of fairies materializing
behind me, "when we get you your true body back,
you'll be able to cock-please her as long as
you'd like."

"Queen Mab," Arthur exclaimed, exiting the tent
and staring from me to her. "Is this… this is why you
returned early?"

"Actually, no," I admitted, and willed the lion out.
It formed nearby, eying the queen of fairies, or
Queen Mab apparently, with a look of suspicion.
"This."

His eyes went wide at that, and Sharon, appeared
groggily from another tent, apparently having been
napping. The others were making their way over.

"Queen Mab, what's the meaning of all this?"
Nivian asked.

"I figured, since someone's stealing my fairies
away from me, I might as well come see what I can
do about it." She held out her arms, as if we were to

worship her then and there, and offered a smile. "So, you all… What can I do about it?"

We shared a look of confusion; Arthur's expression having darkened at her arrival. There was clearly history here, and I couldn't wait to find out what it was.

"Wait. Taking your fairies?" Arthur asked.

Elisa had arrived by that point, just in time to hear what he said. "Actually, I was wondering about the lack of their presence since we arrived." At my look of confusion, she added, "Usually I can sense them, almost feel their power like I do the spirits of my brothers—but it's greatly weakened."

Queen Mab nodded. "She's correct. And I want to know why."

"We don't have the answer to that," Arthur said.

"Well, neither do we," Elisa cut in, holding up a hand. She turned to her older brother, waiting.

He cleared his throat, nodded to Queen Mab in deference. "We've received word from Sekhmet She and Bastet believe they've found something."

"How do we find her?" Queen Mab asked, her eyes narrowed. Another pre-existing set of drama?

"Nivian, do you know where we can find Sekhmet? Can you take us there?" Arthur asked.

"We'll go at once," Nivian replied. "And from

there, get back to this war," her eyes darted to the fairy queen. "Not you, of course."

"For now," Elisa cut in.

"Your brothers found something?" Arthur asked, eyes full of hope.

"Actually, Sekhmet again. A different way, in theory. If Shades are using the portals, you might be able to as well."

"Dark portals," Arthur pointed out. "I'd go through… full shadow."

"Maybe."

This lingered on everyone's minds for a moment, and then he nodded. "Everyone pack up, it's time to …

As we walked, the brother said, "Unless you—us too… unless we went through as gods."

"Jack," Sharon whispered, stepping up shyly.

I took her in my arms, kissed her on the forehead, and laughed. "What's with the hesitation?"

She blushed. "You're different."

"No I'm not. I mean, yes, leveled up and all, but," her hand went to the spot where my lion tattoo was, the lion having retreated back into it, "this is a game changer."

"Is it?"

She nodded, then turned to see Nivian walking on the other side of me.

"A spirit animal, of this kind." Nivian shook her head. "Hasn't happened since Ra."

"Ra was… here?" I asked. "Like this?"

"Ra wasn't always a god," Nivian explained. "Well, this Ra, I mean."

"This Ra?"

"The one who holds the name of Ra," she glanced over to Red.

Red sighed. "We told him about how the myth names can be taken over. I'm guessing he's just not processing all this related to the gods, yet."

"Oh, so it's the same?" I grinned. "Why didn't you just say so?"

"Right." Nivian looked irritated, but Arthur gave her a nod to continue. "Are you sure? Maybe you should tell it."

"It's too close to home," Arthur replied.

"Very well." She turned back to me. "This one was known as… but he learned Ra's secret name, used it to tame the spirit animal of Ra's and therefore, much as you saw Riak become Morgana, he became Ra."

"But I don't understand," I said to Arthur. "Why's that… too close to home?"

Nivian started to explain, but Arthur held up a hand.

"It's okay," he said. "You see, Ra was here with me

at the time. The two of us were like brothers… and he was a big part of what got me through each day."

"What… happened?" I asked.

"A man who claimed to fight evil, after having realized being a real 'boy' hadn't been enough. A man named Pinocchio." Arthur sighed. "He claimed he came in search of me, to find a cure, to help me return. Sought me out and trained with me, befriended me… and then betrayed me for power."

Mists and green, rolling hills gave way to a walkway atop a mountain ridge, stopping for breaks and watching as a herd of hippogriffs flew by. My lion rode out to meet them, playfully circling while we watched and laughed. Apparently, the lion maintained its own will, coming and going as it wanted in addition to when I called upon it.

When the lion returned to my newest tattoo, we packed up, and were on our way again. More lakes, some with strange, curved boats that reminded me of slivers of the moon, and trees of bright purple. When their leaves flew off like cherry blossom petals, they would circle up and take on a life of their own, flittering about, moving to surround us, then disperse into the sunset sky.

"It's all so magical," I said, watching and partly wishing we could stay forever to be part of this, or at least a bit longer to see the many other wonders.

Pucky gave me a pleasant smile, horns glowing for a moment before fading again.

"What?" I asked.

"You did it." She shrugged. "I'm… proud of you."

"Okay, Mom."

She frowned. "Huh?"

"That… came out wrong. I meant… shit. I meant because my mom was always the type to say stuff like that."

"Oh." She stood a bit taller. "I think I'll like your mom."

Actually, the topic reminded me why it was important to return, why, as great as lingering here seemed on the surface, this wasn't my place.

"Will we get to see her? And my dad?" I asked.

Arthur glanced back. "First, make sure they're safe by defeating Ra, but then? Yes, I'd say it's about time."

The idea of walking back into my old place and seeing their beaming faces filled me with joy. A different type of magic.

"When it's over, I'm getting a chimichanga," Sharon said with a silly grin.

"A what?" Queen Mab asked.

"Oooh, you've never had one? Best thing in the world—take a burrito and fry it. Boom! Chimichanga."

"Burrito…?"

Sharon stared at her in disbelief.

"You're in for a good time," I said to the queen, chuckling at Sharon's obsession with chimichangas. They were amazing, sure, but I looked forward to a bacon cheeseburger more than anything, really.

The queen's eyes went from me to Sharon, then Pucky, and she smiled knowingly. "We'll see."

"I didn't mean…"

Pucky put a hand on my arm. "Just let it go. Pretend it never happened."

I nodded, staring forward.

Before long we were entering one of those purple forests, and I was pleased to see Sekhmet walking toward us. What I didn't expect, though, was the way her eyes lit up at seeing me, or how she ran pounced, and tackled me to the ground. At first I started to struggle, but then realized she was sniffing my chest, the spot where my new tattoo was.

She looked up at me with her lioness eyes, and I got it. "Oh, yeah. We have a new friend."

Releasing the lion in a burst of light, I grinned at the way Sckhmet pulled back, crouching, and Bastet the cat curled up around her leg, both staring at my lion in awe.

"Does he… have a name?" Sekhmet asked.

I turned to the lion, cocked my head, and said, "Do you?"

He appeared amused, but merely roared.

"There you go," I said, chuckling. "Sekhmet, Bastet, I'd like you to meet Roar."

"That's not… funny," Sekhmet said. "But I kinda like it."

The lion approached her, let her run her hands through his mane, along his wings, and then turned back to nuzzle me.

"Are the Swan Brothers back from their mission? Have you seen them yet?" Arthur asked.

Sekhmet, almost unable to take her eyes off the lion, finally smiled and nodded. "They're just over there, waiting at the portal."

We all turned to see the direction she indicated, only now realizing there was indeed a spot among the trees darker than the rest. The purple forest provided plenty of shade, but this was more like what I'd seen before, like the ones I'd seen in the mists.

"Why couldn't we use the ones in the mists?" I asked, already guessing at the answer.

"Too dangerous," one of the swan brothers said,

approaching and having heard my question. "Likely already connected to key output points."

"And this?"

"We think the other side is calling their forces, but doing so randomly. If there were any on their side nearby, this might be where they'd go through, but we've been watching it and haven't seen anyone yet."

Sekhmet nodded. "I've been here, too, and haven't seen any Shades or other creatures going through."

"But it's possible all portals lead to the same spot on the other side?" Pucky asked.

"Your guess is as good as ours."

"And there's more," Sekhmet said, turning to Arthur. "I've been trying to figure this out, to remember my past. It's... coming back to me."

"How?" he asked.

She turned to Bastet, who looked at us, took a moment, then opened her mouth and spoke. "It would seem I can talk here in the Fae realm."

We all stared.

Finally, Sekhmet cleared her throat, nodding to her sister. "Go on."

"My memory came back quicker than my sister's. See, we're gods, like Ra, right?"

"Says you," Pucky replied with a hint of scorn. "You're fairy tales like the rest of us."

"No," Bastet turned to her pointedly. "We *were* just like you. But as Arthur knows, his friend became Ra, right? But that's not the only way it can be done."

"That's what we're trying to tell you, Arthur," Sekhmet cut back in. "We know where to get the Golden Goose. Her eggs contain a magic that can bring you back, that can turn you into a god."

He blinked, looked at Nivian, then shook his head. "To take that, if you're right… it would make me a different person."

"I don't think so. Not if your heart is pure."

"Pure?" Arthur laughed. "I'm a fucking vampire!"

"Actually, you're not," Sekhmet pointed out. "While you might still have the vampire powers, because of your status here, I think the curse has been countered."

He considered this, feeling his mouth. "Well, I'll be dammed."

"No, you won't," Sekhmet said, grinning wide now in a way that showed off her own sharp teeth. "You'll be saved, thanks to us."

"Wait, but…" I scratched my chin, more confused than ever now, and in the process realizing I'd grown quite the stubble. "So we not only have to go back and stop Ra, we have to steal a Golden Goose?"

"Correction," Bastet said. "In order to stop Ra, because we'll need all the help we can get," she nodded at Arthur, then the swan brothers, "we'll steal *the* Golden Goose."

"Great. How?"

Sekhmet and Bastet were quiet on this one, looking at each other, than each of us.

"You know where it is?" Red asked.

Bastet nodded. "Hekate will, anyway. Last we heard, the witches had it."

"Chris!" I exclaimed. "So he can help us get it?"

"It would be locked away, behind strong magic," Sekhmet countered. "Even if they know where it is, it'll take some doing."

"Only one person I know who can get past any traps and locks, no matter how much magic is put to trying to keep her out." Red turned to Pucky, then Elisa. "We've got to find Goldilocks."

"Ah, fuck," Pucky said, but then laughed. "There goes the neighborhood."

"What?" I asked.

"Don't worry about it."

Red gave me a look, but Elisa spoke up. "Anytime Pucky's ever been interested in a guy, Goldilocks would try to steal him out from under her nose. And it worked every time."

"Fuck you all," Pucky said, looking my way a bit sheepishly.

"Pucky," I said, stepping up to her and taking her hands. "No matter what, that will not happen here. I promise. Double promise."

She squeezed my hand, chuckled, and looked away. "I'm not worried."

"Good." I kissed her hand. "Because you have no reason to be."

"It's settled then," Nivian said, turning back to Elisa and her brothers now all together once more. "With the connection to Arthur, I believe I have the power to send the main group through the lake, back to the where your hideout is. If I can manage. Elisa, you'll need to be the link point for that. Your brothers will stay here with Arthur and the fairy queen."

"I think my sister and I should go through the portal," Sekhmet cut in.

"It's too dangerous," Nivian replied.

"Exactly. We go through, see where it leads, and then find our way back to the team. Way I see it, we're the most likely to survive whatever's on the other side, and worst case scenario can fake our way out of there. We'll know where the other side is, and when it's time to come back for you all, we'll be able to use the portal as a passage point."

Nivian considered this, turning to Arthur. "She makes a good point, and sending you all through the lake might not even work as gods."

Arthur nodded. "So shall it be."

"We have a plan, then," Elisa said. "Meanwhile, we find the witches to get the location, for Goldilocks to steal the goose, and then we'll make Arthur and my brothers gods."

"And get me out of here, too," the fairy queen added."

"Sure."

"Fucking awesome," Sharon said, and for the first time I noticed how giddy she was.

"What're you so excited about?" I asked with a laugh.

"Oh, just getting to fuck over the bad guys. I've been looking forward to getting some payback."

I laughed, nodding. "Let's do it then."

We wished Elisa's brothers and Arthur well, leaving them with promises of sending for them all soon, and made our way back to the lake, leaving them there to set up camp and Sekhmet to go through the portal with her sister.

It took some time to make it back to the lake, but when we were there, all of us were silent, solemn, ready for the adventure ahead.

"Focus," Nivian said to me, guiding us to lean over, to look into the water.

We stared into the lake, at our reflections, and as Nivian slid into the water, legs becoming a fish tail, the reflection rippled. The Fae landscape faded to that of our Earth, to the mansion where I'd first learned of Elisa and her painting. Where I'd started out life as a Protector.

Then it wasn't a reflection anymore, but we were there, in the pool where I'd enjoyed the company of my ladies.

Home at last.

13

My first instinct was to turn on the news to see what we missed, while Red probably had the better idea of pulling up Mowgli on the comms. I watched in horror unable to take my eyes away as the television showed images of much of Europe in ruins.

"You…you're alive," Mowgli said.

"Sorry we couldn't be in touch earlier," Red replied. "We were in the Fae realm."

"And everything there's as it should be?"

Red hesitated as an image showed a crater where Stone Henge had once stood for untold years, cities in ruins like looking like the aftermath of Hiroshima.

"No." Red stepped over next to me, the floating

screen with Mowgli's face at her side. "First, we found Queen Mab, or Jack did."

I waved, eyes darting between Mowgli and the destruction.

"Glad to see you alive and well," Mowgli said.

"Thank you. You too, sir."

He chuckled. "So, Queen Mab? How?"

"I guess she found me."

"And…" Red nudged me, made a flapping motion with her hand.

"Ah, right. And… I got a spirit animal."

"Well blow me down," Mowgli said in his best Popeye impersonation. At my look, he shook his head. "Sorry, and no, Popeye isn't one of us. Doesn't exist outside of cartoons, unfortunately."

I chuckled. "That's too bad."

"What sort of spirit animal, if I may?" He was leaning closer to the screen, his excitement evident. It made sense, if what they told me was true about how rare spirit animals truly were.

"A flying lion and…" I touched my heart. "He's resting, at the moment."

Mowgli looked at me with a whole new level of respect.

Meanwhile, on the news, a woman appeared floating over the Louvre, her yellow robes flapping in the wind as the military sent a barrage of shots her way. Cannon, guns, you name it. None of it did a damn thing, and when she clapped her hands together, an explosion sent them all back, destroying the glass pyramids of the Louvre.

"Shit," I said under my breath. "We wasted too much time."

"As far as Earth is concerned, we've barely been gone at all," Elisa replied.

"About an hour," Mowgli clarified. "And yes, that's still too long. Ra and the others have already managed to take out much of Europe, and they're spreading, calling on all the fairy tales to join their side, telling humans to bow down in worship. It's bad."

Elisa stepped up to join us. "My brothers are working with Arthur. They think Queen Mab can bring them back, like Ra."

"That's good news."

"And you?" she asked. "I suppose there's a plan."

He grimaced. "We lost a lot, we—"

"Fell back…" Red said, voice cold.

"Er, yes." He looked ashamed. "We just don't have the forces, Red."

"Others are falling," Sharon said, and I turned to see her, a grim expression, eyes partly shadowed. "I feel them."

I took her hand, squeezing it. "Don't."

She blinked, clearing the shadow away. "I had to know."

"How bad?" Elisa asked.

"Bad…"

"She's right," Mowgli confirmed. "I wouldn't know as well as she, but we've been reaching out to our worldwide network, and all along Europe up to Russia has fallen or gone over. We suspect many have gone over to the other side."

A nod from Sharon.

"We're going to need every ally we can get," Pucky said. "And already have plans in that regard."

Elisa sighed. "The witches."

Mowgli nodded, but his eyes darted off to the side.

"What is it?" Red asked.

"They've been… out of contact." Mowgli faced us again. "Jack, how much do you trust this friend of yours?"

"Chris?" I asked. "Like a brother. The good kind, not the stab you in the back kind. But…"

"What?"

"If pus—I mean, if women are involved, every-thing tends to go out the window with him. And in this case, we know women are."

"Only one way to find out," Elisa interjected.

"Time to pay our friends a little visit. I'll make contact, see what we can find."

She went off to make her calls, leaving us to clean up, eat and hydrate, and then pass our time until word came on where we'd meet up.

Every minute we spent waiting to hear from Chris and the witches was another filling me with dread, making me worry that he'd turned. We moved to the main living room, putting the news on a larger projector, and decided that if we hadn't heard from them within the hour, we'd make do on our own... somehow. Or at least go down fighting, rather than hiding out waiting to hear from someone who might be on the other side.

God, I hoped he hadn't turned.

"Tense?" Elisa asked, eyeing me.

"Of course I'm fucking tense!" I blew up, took a deep breath, and then held up my hands. "Sorry, I... yes."

She nodded to the back room. "Painting always calms my nerves."

"Painting?" Sharon asked, confused.

Elisa nodded, turning back my way.

"Which kind of painting?" I asked.

"Your choice." Elisa looked over to Sharon, the two there looking like complete opposites—the former prim and proper, Sharon wild as hell.

There wasn't much choice in this, as long as Sharon was on board. And since the others were occupied, I nodded, already going for the bedroom.

"You've never tried painting, Sharon?"

"No, I was always busy trying to maintain my sanity. Turned to exercise, boxing mostly… rock climbing."

Elisa took her hand. "You'll love it."

Sharon appeared skeptical, but when she saw the look in my eyes as I waited for her, she took on that look like she knew something was up.

As soon as we entered the room, it was clear Elisa had already had this in mind. The paints were all set up, her mischievous smile spreading wide.

"How does this work?" Sharon asked, arms folded over her chest.

"Stripping would be a good first step," Elisa said, already moving over to start mixing colors. She eyed the woman, frowning slightly to see she wasn't moving to take off her clothes right away. "Unless you feel uncomfortable and would rather go watch the news some more."

Sharon pursed her lips, looked at me, then Elisa. "No, no… I'll stay."

"Good. Now take it off, girl."

Sharon still looked hesitant, so I stepped over. "Maybe it's more fun if I help."

Elisa watched us, brush in hand, pausing from her painting, as I started to lift Sharon's shirt.

"It's torn anyway," Elisa pointed out. "And I've already sent out for new clothes for her, so…"

I got what she was saying, and gave Sharon a look to make sure she was okay with this. She nodded, so instead I tore the shirt off, leaving it hanging then did the same with her pants. She laughed, looked at Elisa nervously, then let her claws extend and did the same to me, leaving me nude with my clothes in shreds on the floor.

"Oh, well," Elisa shrugged. "I hadn't ordered any for him, but we can figure it out. Think some of the guards will have some clothes lying around."

"Now you tell us," I said, grinning.

It wasn't the time to worry about not having clothes though, because Sharon and I were nude. Elisa set her paintbrush aside to strip as well, and soon the three of us were on the bed, kissing, caressing, moaning. Elisa ran her hand down between Sharon's legs, eyes on me, and then kissed the woman's neck.

"Take over," she told me, moving back to retrieve the paints. As I did, hands on Sharon's ass and pulling her over and on top of me, Elisa analyzed us like a canvas. Sharon reached between us to caress my balls, then ran her hand up my shaft, playing with the tip. My lips had just pressed to her nipple when she yelped and arched her back, Elisa having apparently applied a generous amount of paint along her spine, down to the crack of her ass.

"Keep going," Elisa said, earning a very confused —but intrigued—look from Sharon.

"You two are into this?" Sharon asked.

"Very much so," I replied. I'd only really gotten into it once, and it had been so wild, so different, I was pleased to be sharing the experience with her.

Elisa cleared her throat and nodded to the corner, where I now saw a large pot of steaming water, a bottle of soap next to it. She'd apparently had the servants bring in a bath in the old style for us to be clean during all this. I felt clean enough, but Sharon had her thing, and was already moving away and into it. The image of her in that old bath hadn't been something I'd expected to turn me on so much, but somehow imagining her in the Wild West bathing like this did it. I was over in a flash, helping to wash her ass. As soon as she was out, I bent her over and gave her what she wanted—a nice tongue job on the asshole.

"Now there's a fucking sight to behold," Elisa said. I'd forgotten that she hadn't been part of this experience before.

Sharon turned, moaning and watching as Elisa

came over, paint brush caressing her ass. Next, Elisa licked the forefinger of her other hand and then slowly inserted it into Sharon's ass. "No, thank you, I prefer this."

Right there, she started fingering her ass, and Sharon was into it. I watched for a moment, but then Elisa motioned me to the bath, sticking her tongue in her cheek in a way that made it clear what she wanted. So I did, moving over and lowering myself into the water, then standing so that my dick was there in Sharon's face.

"What, you want me to huff, and puff, and…" Sharon grinned up at me, waiting for me to finish the phrase.

"Corny," I said, laughing.

"What, you thought I'd say something about blowing?" She winked. "My actions speak louder than words."

She eyed it, bit her lip and then opened her mouth. In her position, with Elisa still fingering her ass, she couldn't exactly use her hands or she'd fall, so I guided it in, like an airplane coming in for a landing. She seemed unsure, at first, but then was licking it, bobbing her head slightly. And then she had her tongue twirling around my tip like an ice cream, before taking me in fully. Oh, God, her mouth felt good, that warmth against the cold of the mists. I went full on fun mode, took her by her wild mane, and started moving with the motion.

"That's more like it," Elisa said, grinning wide as she took her other hand and, I couldn't see, but based on Sharon's increased moans and intensity of sucking my cock, she'd started fingering her pussy now, too.

When Sharon had her first orgasm, Elisa slapped her once on the ass, then went over to wash her hands as I took Sharon and threw her back on the bed. Elisa was getting more paints ready before joining us, while I moved my cock into position with Sharon, her hairy pussy a bit coarse on the outside, warm and moist on the inside as I slid in.

As I thrust, flicks of paint hit me, then a paint brush was on Sharon's nipple, painting one pink, the next purple, making them eyes of a smiley face with a long stroke for the smile.

I laughed. "Quit joking around."

Elisa stepped back, grinned, and then straddled Sharon's face. "Does our new friend eat out much?"

In that position I couldn't see Sharon, except to tell that she'd gone stiff. Clearly uncomfortable. I was about to say something as I brought my thrusting to a slow, love making rhythm, but then Sharon's tongue flicked out. She tenderly tasted Elisa, and then was suddenly all into it. Fuck that was hot, causing me to get into my thrusting with such vigor that soon it became difficult for us all to stay in place, and Elisa fell over.

She was laughing then, pushing Sharon away and squirming, apparently having fallen mid-orgasm, and then Sharon moved aside and thrust me toward Elisa.

"My turn to paint," she said, and grabbed handfuls of blue and red, running them up my back and across Elisa's breasts as I now took Elisa and began making love to her.

She pulled me close, moaning and whispering, "Slow, slow… oh, gentle…" and then was moaning and punching the bed, finally finishing with one long, blissful release.

Sharon jumped back on right away, but made a face and said, "Fuck, it's sensitive, let's just…"

A glance around and she wiped the rest of the paint on my chest, or as much as she could, and then took my cock with both hands, stroking it vigorously. I leaned back, thrust my hips forward, and enjoyed the feel of it until I unleashed all over her arms and stomach.

She laughed, rolled over, and caught her breath.

"The painting isn't over," Elisa said, apparently having recovered, and she pushed me over, dabbing her brush into the paint.

Elisa was lying over me, her paintbrush tickling as she painted little Celtic designs on my cock, Sharon biting her lip as she watched.

"The funny part is how they'll change shape when it shrinks," Elisa said, more as if commenting on art than on my body.

"Too bad I'm such a grower, or we wouldn't have to worry about it," I replied, propping my head up to get a better look. She really was quite the artist.

"You are a *major* grower," Sharon commented.

"Hey." I frowned, not sure if I should take that as a compliment or insult. There wasn't time to figure it out, though, because a light shot out as a portal opened right next to the bed. As we all turned in confusion, a young witch stepping out. She froze, staring at us lying there nude and covered in paint. She cocked her head at the Celtic designs on my dick, and nodded, clearly impressed.

"If this is why you all called for Chris, I feel obliged to tell you, he's in a bit of a relationship. Kind of."

"No, no," I said, sitting up and taking the sheet to cover myself. "Damn, sorry. We were just waiting and—"

"Got to painting. Yes, I see that."

I grinned, looking to Sharon and Elisa, who were both trying not to crack up.

"Anyway, did you want to… get dressed or…?" The witch motioned to the portal.

"Or go like this?" Elisa asked, gesturing to her nude body, covered in yellow and green strokes of paint. "I think we'll need a couple of minutes."

"Isn't the world under attack?"

"Fine, thirty seconds."

"Thirty seconds?" I asked.

She was already up, motioning me along to the bathroom while the witch waited.

"Red!" Elisa called out, voice carrying through the halls.

"Don't fucking shout for me!" Red shouted.

"I'm not. Just letting you know we have company," Elisa smiled, turned on the shower, and motioned us in. "Quickly now, scrub each other off. Help me get to those hard to reach areas."

I grinned, getting in the shower and grabbing the bottle of soap, starting to quickly lather myself up, then Sharon. She got Elisa as she entered, and in a few seconds of sensual caressing and washing, we were back out. We dried off and found our new clothes,

"This… is odd," I said, holding up the dress pants and dress shirt a guard had set aside for me, thankfully. "I'll look like my dad about to go do some banking."

"I think it'll be hot," Pucky said, entering with Red.

Red nodded, then looked around at the paint-covered sheets and walls.

"Seriously?" Red said, turning to the witch as if to apologize, but the witch held up a hand to stop her.

"Trust me," the witch said, "what you all have going here is *nothing* compared to what Chris has been doing."

"Color me curious." I pulled on my pants, then the shirt, leaving it untucked. "Let's go ask him all about it."

"Or maybe focus on more important matters," Elisa said with a laugh.

14

We followed this witch through the portal that led to a valley covered with trees on each side. At the bottom, where we were, was a field with a hedge maze twice as tall as myself, and a tall New Orleans looking mansion large enough for several families visible on the far side.

"Where's Chris?" I asked.

"He'll be with Hekate, to be sure," the witch said. "They sent me ahead while they finished up. Hopefully, they'll be decent."

"Decent…" I repeated the word, not as a question, but as a realization. He had, I was guessing, fallen into the same pattern I'd become accustomed to. Training, fighting, fucking. It wasn't a bad life, and judging by the fact that he was with Hekate, and seeing this little number, I had no doubt he was happy with how it'd turned out.

She led us back across a neatly manicured lawn with a circular fountain in the middle, and through the entrance into the hedge maze, headed towards the mansion on the far side. , She glanced over and grinned at me.

"What?" I asked.

"It's just, you look a lot cooler than Chris makes you out to be."

"The hell?"

She laughed. "It's a compliment, really. You know, with the way it used to be so hard for you to meet girls and all. He told us about this one time—"

"Maybe we don't need to talk while we walk?"

"Come on," Pucky said, laughing. "Let the lady talk."

I growled, but waved her on.

"It's nothing, really," the little witch said. "He thought it was funny. I mean, I don't have to tell them."

"Whatever."

She skipped along, leading us through the next part of the maze, where it turned several times so that I would've sworn we were going in a circle, except that nothing looked familiar.

"That time on the beach," she said. "You went

there thinking you'd be meeting this girl you'd overheard at school saying she was going, but apparently you went to the wrong one. Stayed all day and got sunburned."

"He was there with me," I mumbled.

"Or what about the time you got caught touching yourself in Crystal's bathroom?" She laughed. "Hilarious."

"He…" I blushed, not even sure how he knew about that. I'd only ever told… nobody. "I'd had a major crush on her, didn't want my boner bothering me and giving it away, so figured there was only one way to get rid of it."

My ladies had a mixture of humor and uncertainty on their faces.

"Oh come on, I was like fifteen at the time, and he wasn't' supposed to know about that. The only thing I can think is that she told him, but I don't get why."

"Because they were dating at the time."

I stopped, staring, mouth open. "Shit, how did I never see that."

She winked. "Sometimes you don't see something right in front of you, if you don't want to see it."

The next turn led us to an open area where a picnic was laid out on a grassy field, three naked bodies there on the lawn.

"I'm trying not to see it," I said to the witch. "What you said… it's not working."

"I did say 'sometimes,'" she replied with a laugh.

Chris was one of them, naturally. He was bent backwards over a pile of clothes on a rock, some random witch rubbing his cock between her overly large breasts while Hekate stood over his mouth so that he could eat her out. The weirdest part wasn't even that, but how she had various colored candles on a bench next to him, and at the moment was pouring candle wax onto his flesh from a pink candle. His body convulsed as it hit but already had green and purple hardened in lines along his body.

"Dude," was all I could say.

He held up a hand, not stopping. Hekate smiled at us, adjusted herself so that he better had her clit, and moaned long and loud before stepping away.

"Finish him, Mirna," she said with a shrug.

Chris tried to push himself up, but in that moment Mirna, looking our way and blushing, started working him hard with two hands so that he collapsed back as his cum shot out onto his belly.

I turned away in disgust, glad to see my team of ladies had been a step ahead of me, already with their backs to the situation.

"Could've just told us to wait," I called over my shoulder.

"Fuck…" Chris said, voice heavy with exhaustion. "Fuck that."

He was up and walking toward us, I could tell in my periphery, so I risked a glance to see that he was wiping himself off with a witch's gown. He tossed it aside, then stood there nude but for the candle wax, grinning wide.

"So?" he asked. "What'ya think?"

"I think you need to get some clothes on."

He laughed, waving my comment off. "No, I mean about this place. Isn't it amazing?"

"It's different,"

"I don't like it," Sharon said.

He put his hand to his chin, looking up at the mansion. Now that I really noticed it, too, it had that dark aura to it that I could understand Sharon being against.

"Yeah, a bit dreary I guess," Chris said. "But you get used to it."

"Know what I can't get used to?" I asked, annoyed when I saw Elisa glance down at him. "You without pants."

Chris guffawed, but then turned and started looking for his pants, while Hekate came over.

"For the record," Elisa said, "I wasn't looking there. More appreciating the candle wax art."

"Uh huh."

"It's part of some magic I was trying on him," Hekate explained. Now it was my turn to try to not look, because she was as naked as him. The other witch, a shorter woman with wild blue hair, grinned over at us as she tried to fit her breasts into a bra. It looked like a challenge.

Pucky cleared her throat.

"I wasn't looking either," I explained, but blushed. "Just…"

"He was looking," Sharon said, arms crossed.

"Not in that way," I countered.

"Shut up and enjoy the show," Pucky said with a laugh. "I'm not judging, because I know you're coming home with me, not them."

"Your friend's got a big cock, but it's funny look-ing," Red said. When the other girls turned to her, she shrugged. "Yeah, I looked, why the fuck wouldn't I? There's a cock hanging out, my eyes are going to observe. Doesn't mean anything."

I laughed at that, and shrugged. She had a point—I'd been looking at those massive titties, at Hekate's tight body and shaved pussy. But it wasn't that I wanted either of them. I had more women than I could handle. But when breasts and pussy are out there for the eyes to roam over, they're going to roam.

Moving on, I turned back to Hekate and Chris. "Tell me you're aware of what's going on out there."

Chris had just pulled on a pair of boxers, and was now finding his pants. "Yeah, that's what the spell was for. Protection. We were getting ready to go on the offensive."

"Before or after you heard from us?" Red asked.

He frowned at her, then turned back to me. "The thing was—"

"Did he just ignore me because I said his dong was funny looking?"

Chris glared at her, nodded curtly, and then said, "As I was saying, I've managed to get a few of the witches on our side."

"Five," the short one called out, voice higher pitched than I would've thought.

She, at least, was finally pulling a robe over herself. Only, as I cringed to see, it was the one Chris had been wiping himself with. She looked down and saw it too, cursed, and pulled it right back off. I quickly looked away.

"Okay, five witches," Elisa said, folding her hands together. "We can work with that, I think."

"And are we in a witch den or something?" I asked.

"This place?" Chris chuckled. "Shit, son, don't

you know? I had her open a portal here for a reason —we're in the heart of it."

"What do you mean?"

He pulled on his shirt now, finally fully dressed minus socks and shoes. "Right out there—not far off, is the catacombs. We go up here, we're going to be in the heart of it."

"Except…" Elisa frowned. "We don't want to be in the heart of it. We need to find the Golden Goose."

"The fuck you do," Hekate said, staring her down. "It ain't going to happen."

"You want to explain to Nivian that Arthur is stuck in the Fae lands forever?" Red said. "Or…" She turned to Elisa, who stepped forward.

"Or try telling me you're going to keep my brothers there as well, knowing there's a way to avoid it?"

Hekate frowned at her, licked her lips, then sighed. "Fuck."

"So you'll do it?"

"We're going to need to go into the mansion, where we'll have information on how to find it, though of course it's not there itself. You wait here and—"

"Not going to happen," Elisa countered. "We're going with you."

Hekate opened her mouth to protest, but clearly thought better of it. With a nod toward the mansion and a worried look Chris's way, she said, "Looks like it's time to give them a tour."

The worry in Chris's eyes made my heart thud at the thought, but it was the next step in our journey, and a necessary one.

"Come on then," Mirna said, gesturing to us. "We'll need to cast an illusionary spell on the lot of you, and hope it holds. Because if not…"

"We're all going to be fucked," Chris finished for her.

15

Mirna and the other two witches quickly had us glamoured, with the help of the blue candles and some spell casting. Chris actually joined in the chant, a small bit of purple light coming from his fingertips as the spell had moved over us, making us all appear in the purple and black robes the witches mostly wore here.

"Not all witches dress that way, but it's a sort of uniform when in the coven," Hekate explained. "At least, this coven."

"And they live here," I asked. "Or is this like some school of witchcraft and wizardry?"

"A what?" Hekate asked, frowning.

Chris chuckled. "She's just giving you a hard time. I asked the same thing—but no, no such things.

This is more like a crazy cult, most of the witches here actually worshipping Hekate."

"It's not a cult," Hekate countered. "And they only worship me in that they think I'm amazing. If I told them all to switch sides right now, we'd maybe get one or two out of the bunch."

"Why don't you?" I asked.

"Because the rest would turn on her," Pucky explained. "And then we'd have to fight them all off."

"Kill 'em," Sharon added. When the others looked at her, she shrugged. "It's true. We'd be able to take them, but I imagine Hekate feels a special something here. No? Otherwise, why not?"

Hekate grunted, not saying anything more on the subject, and therefore confirming what Sharon had suggested. Either way, I was enjoying walking up the curved steps leading up to the mansion, knowing that I hadn't had to drink any strange potions with people's hair in them or whatever to get this look of being someone else. It was odd, seeing Red and the others in a way that almost made them look like stranger, but not quite. Something about the spell allowed us to sort of see the new version as a layer on top of the old, like a strange veneer covering the real us. We looked bizarre, I thought with a grin.

"What're you smirking about?" Sharon asked as we reached the door.

Realizing how difficult this must be for her—entering a place that was not only part of the whole shadow world, but that embraced it full on—I wiped away my smile. Stepping aside, I held out an arm like I'd escort her in.

"Not here," Hekate said, brushing past us and slamming my arm away.

"Gotta act the part," Chris said as he followed.

Suddenly the fact that he'd survived this place and likely even started to fit in all made sense. He was my friend, but had always been a major douche. I nodded, standing a little taller and looking down my nose as stuck up asses often did, and followed. At least my new attitude earned a little chuckle from Pucky.

The mansion took on a whole new level of darkness once we were inside. Not that it was dark in the visibility sense, as there were candles burning along the walls, torches at the far end at the sides of the two staircases. But the paintings were all dreary, of snakes and dead trees and strange circles with patterns—some glowing unnaturally.

As much as they were trying to tell me this wasn't something out of Harry Potter, I couldn't help feeling this would've been what Voldemort's house would've looked like if he'd retired.

"I think I'll wait outside," Sharon whispered.

Red caught her arm. "We can't split up. Not in a place like this."

Hekate gave her a brief nod. "Stick close, you'll be fine. It's the others we have to worry about."

"How's that?" Elisa asked, glaring.

"She's at least closer on the spectrum. You all ooze goodness like a toddler's runny nose that first week at daycare. It's disgusting."

"Thanks," Elisa replied, taking the lead, but pausing between the two stairwells.

"Always left," Mirna whispered, helpfully.

"Because it's the opposite of what's right," Pucky said with a grin.

"No, because your left side of the brain is more logical," Mirna said. "Deals with science. In the end, witchcraft all starts at a point with science."

"And for the record, there are good witches," Hekate hissed, clearly offended.

Pucky pretended to zip her mouth, tossing the key behind her.

We made our way up the stairs to the left, a winding, marble staircase that led to a hallway. Long and dark, with tiled floors and gilded gold trim along the ceiling. Speaking of the ceiling, as we walked along I noticed a mural of the witch trials stretching all along the length of it, and what seemed to be pictures depicting various events in witching history.

"Where is everyone?" I asked as we passed several empty rooms and connecting halls.

"Many are off fighting," Hekate said. "Some are here, refusing to join in the war."

"But I'd think the witches would be the first to join Ra."

"You'd think wrong," Chris interjected. "Think of it this way—chaotic evil, or some chaotic neutral. And the chaotic part often wins out, in the case of these groups, so…"

"When did you learn to speak nerd?" I asked.

He laughed. "That'd be all thanks to Mirna. Got me playing table top games in the evening."

"Figured it was the best way to help him understand what's what," Mirna offered with a proud smile. "Meanwhile, the fucker didn't even come calling," "Oh, not that I would've accepted if he had, of course. But still, it's nice to know people want your skills. Or gods want… you know what I mean."

Pucky laughed, then covered her mouth with a glance at our surroundings. "For me, knowing that I'm on the side of what's right is enough."

"Says the nature lover," Mirna replied. "If it weren't for Chris and his sweet-talking ways, I honestly don't know if I'd be on this side or not."

"What?" I said, looking from her to Chris.

"I mean it, how do I know you all are actually on the right side."

I shook my head. "I was surprised at the mention of Chris and sweet talking, that's all."

Chris chuckled and shot me a glance. "You forget who always had the luck with the ladies."

"That so?" Hekate asked, nudging him.

Elisa cleared her throat. "Maybe we focus on the task at hand, then compare notes on who's sweet and who was able to get all the ladies."

"Or wasn't either," Chris nodded my way, but then held up his hands. "Sure, sure. Of course."

She gave him a pointed look, so he stepped back, turning to Hekate. She'd stopped at a hallway to our right, gesturing us over.

"It'll be this way, but…" She held up a hand, then cursed under her breath. "Back—there."

Following her indication that we move to the next hall over, we quickly found ourselves in one of the side rooms. Judging by the mirror and desk, it was nothing more than a powder room, or so I thought until Chris stood between me and the mirror and pulled a curtain over it.

"Best not look into those," he said. "Not in a place like this."

"And not with how the glamour makes him look,"

Sharon added. At my scowl, she frowned and said, "What? I like the real you, not… this."

She actually looked kinda hot in her glamour, but I wasn't about to say that. Not more attractive than normal—because that was hard to beat—just different.

"Someone's out there," Elisa hissed from the doorway with Hekate.

The witch nodded, glancing back and then shooing her away. "That's right, so keep it quiet."

I nodded, scooting back but bumping into Red. There wasn't much room in there with all of us crammed in. She didn't mind, and put an arm around my waist as she whispered into my ear, "Nice and cozy."

The dirty part of my mind wondered if she was trying to come on to me in this place. It wouldn't be the first time that a 'dangerous situation' had turned on one of these ladies, but there was something about Chris being in there that totally killed it for me. Maybe it was the fact that I'd now seen him in two sexual situations, both of which had been odd enough to leave my retinas scarred, or at least my mind. Even just standing there I couldn't help seeing Hekate and remembering the first time we'd found him with her doing something to his ass—I tried not to think about it.

"We just wait them out?" Pucky asked. "Or…"

"If you're thinking you'd rather charge out there, dicks swinging," Mirna said, shaking her head, "give up that line of thought right now. We're hardly the most powerful witches in this place, and the house works in mysterious ways."

"Speak for yourself," Hekate countered. "I'd put my powers up against any one of them."

Mirna gave her a skeptical glance, then shrugged. "Yeah, maybe."

Hekate looked offended, but left it alone.

"Aren't we all glamoured anyway?" I asked. "Shouldn't we be able to walk around freely, or what was the point?"

"From a distance you're safe, but with magic like theirs, getting too close will expose you for sure." Hekate

"Almara," Chris said, and I turned to realize the third, mostly silent, witch, had one of her hands down his pants. The fact was mostly hidden by her robe and long sleeve, but not enough. At my look, Chris tried to cover the fact, and shook his head while hissing, "Not now."

"Looks like his team is as frisky as yours, huh?" Pucky said to me with a wink.

I chuckled.

"One level below, I'd say," Mirna interjected. "Otherwise, one of you would be—"

"This isn't the time or place," Hekate said, and then waved her hand. In a flash, all of our voices were cut off. I even tried to say something, and no sound came out.

We stared at her in horror, and she smiled back smugly. Her hand went to the door to prop it open slightly and have a look.

"We might be in the clear," she whispered, "but can't go risking it with you all—shit!"

She pulled back, eyes wide, and quickly scanned us all. "Okay, here goes nothing." Eyes roaming over us, she nodded. "Mirna, Alrmara, you two go out and pass them, pretend you're on your way to sparring practice or something of the sort, and maybe they'll have just assumed it was you over here."

We all shared a nervous glance, then moved aside as best we could to let them exit. The silent one had to pull her hand out of Chris's pants to do so, and used that same hand to blow him a kiss.

He gave me a 'what can I do' sort of look, and grinned. Of course, he loved it.

As soon as they exited, a voice spoke up. Husky, but definitely feminine, and with some sort of accent. "The time for inaction is over, gather your coven."

"Yes, of course," Mirna's voice sounded, soft and muffled.

Hekate frowned, staring at the floor with her hand on the door. It didn't strike me though as a real problem until I noticed the glow coming from her hand, moving along the edges of the door, filling in the cracks.

A look from Red and then Pucky showed it wasn't the time to make jokes or even ask what was going on. Sharon was on the opposite side of the room from me and her eyes had a clouded look, one I recognized from our brief training sessions. *Push back the shadow*, my internal voice urged, sounding much like her voice in that moment.

And indeed, there was a darkness around the glow, as if the light from Hekate and a shadow power were fighting each other, each working for domination regarding those doors. I stared at the darkness, watching it shift, change shape, seep through… and I started to walk toward it, pushing my way to the doors.

Red's hand met my chest and I swatted it away, mind reeling with sensations of pain, anger at watching everyone I loved suffer. I froze, closing my eyes and remembering all I'd learned, hand going to my chest.

I had a fucking spirit animal, or familiar or whatever it was called, living in me. A lion with wings. How did some shadow bullshit hope to touch me? No way.

Clenching my jaw, I stepped back. A smile from Sharon, though forced, showed me she had felt the same calling, and overcome it.

And just like that, the shadows were gone.

Hekate turned back to us, sweat on her brow, but also relief.

"Who is it?" Elisa asked, clearly sensing the main part of the danger zone.

"Not one of ours," Hekate replied. "And apparently the idea of us being chaotic no longer matters. They're calling in all possible forces."

"Must have an inkling that we've returned," I said.

Elisa cringed. "Actually, I've been wondering about that. If they have any way of knowing, or sensing."

"I wouldn't assume so," Hekate said. "This might be in relation to the pushback from the normies. When they found out their lead agent and many of his followers were actually Legends or gods in disguise, a lot of the agencies put in place to hunt our kind went into war mode. Now they're trying to exterminate us without worrying about the general populace finding out. They don't care, since Ra and his followers haven't exactly been discrete."

"Meaning they're going to try and exterminate us as quickly as possible," Pucky said, a sour look on her face.

"Exactly."

"But if we can defeat Ra and them first?" I asked.

"It'll help, but not in the grand scheme of things." Red approached the door now, pulling her cloak around her. "We'd best get moving, because they're not going to give us time to sit around."

"One second," Hekate said, listening at the door again.

"Myths are likely dying out there," Red went on. I'm not going to stand around hiding—"

"Don't make me silence you again," Hekate hissed. A moment of silence followed, during which Red's cheeks took on a flush that could have almost matched her cloak. She was just starting to look like she would explode, when the door swung outward, revealing Chris's other two witches.

"Clear," Mirna said, and then nodded.

"Who was it?" Hekate asked.

Mirna hesitated, then grimaced. "Fucking guess."

"No…"

"What?" Pucky asked. "Who?"

I was leaning forward in interest by that point as well.

"Think of one bitch you hear about in all the myths and whatnot, who would you assume?" Hekate asked.

I pursed my lips, then stood straight. "Medusa!"

"What?" Elisa scoffed. "That's just... no, she came over to our side a long time ago."

"Oh... Pandora?"

Elisa just shook her head this time, everyone turning back to Hekate. Yeah, I gave up.

"One hint—mother of the underworld, they called her." Hekate looked to me, hopefully, but I was drawing a blank.

Pucky moved her mouth, but I didn't get it. "Persephone," Pucky whispered my way.

"Ah, Persephone. Didn't she escape the underworld, and..." I scratched my head. "There's a bit of a mumbo-jumbo thing going on in my brain where I'm getting the mythology and the video game stuff confused."

"Doesn't matter," Hekate said. "Because we're talking about reality here, not the stories. Reality is that she's a very powerful Legend, at goddess status, and her shadow magic is fucking badass."

"Ah."

Sharon nodded at me, and for the first time I noticed the worry in her yes.

"You knew her?" I asked Sharon.

"Sure," Sharon replied. "Since she kind of made me evil to begin with."

"Tell him as we go," Hekate said, "if you're going to tell the story. Either way, we need to be moving."

"Seconded," Elisa said, and followed the witches out the door.

As we went back to the hallway Hekate had originally indicated as the way to go, I turned to Sharon and gave her a look of compassion and curiosity.

"It's a tough one," Sharon started.

When she didn't say more, I let it go, continuing on up more stairs and passages, until finally, when Hekate went ahead to scout out the final hallway and I found myself standing close to Sharon, she said, "Do you want to know or not?"

"Of course I do."

"Then ask."

"I…" With a grin and a nod of surrender, I asked, "What happened? Why was it a tough one?"

"She both saved me, and destroyed me." Holding out her hand, she waited until I took it to continue. "I would've died if not for her, as I'd been bitten, see… bitten and discarded, left to die. She found me—"

"How?" I interrupted, then squeezed her hand. "Sorry."

"No, it's okay. I... was sort of on a date. Experimenting with this girl from college, and she took me to this shady bar, took me out back and I thought it would be my first female-on-female kiss. Turns out her friend was there—the Big Bad Wolf of the time. It was apparently a bar a lot of Legends liked to visit, because after the bite and leaving me, I remember seeing Persephone—stepping out, sniffing the air. She gave me the power, but said she'd come to deal with the Big Bad Wolf. Told me I could live if I settled things for her, and then... entrapped me."

"You used this power to kill the old Big Bad Wolf, and therefore took over the name and associated darkness," I said, filling in the rest for her based on where I saw this going.

"She essentially kept me as her slave until... well, until you all freed me."

"You freed yourself."

She scoffed. "Don't feed me that corny bullshit." The look in her eyes was one of affection and appreciation.

"If you meet her again... are you worried?"

A simple nod in response. I took her hand, kissed it, and said, "I'll be here with you. No matter what."

"Pssst," Hekate signaled us, and we all moved

forward to where she stood. There was a cabinet in front of her in a sort of alcove. I was half expecting her to open it and reveal the Golden Goose. Instead, she opened it and moved two bottles near the back, which resulted in a secret passage opening up at the edge of the walls near the window, almost out of sight even if it weren't completely hidden.

"I want this house," I said, having always been fascinated by places with secret entrances. Blame it on *Duck Tales*.

"Already spoken for," Chris said with a grin. "And we've marked our territory on half the secret passages. I didn't know about this one, though."

"Because I'm not an idiot," Hekate said as she led the way. "Taking you here would've been too dangerous. But now we don't really have a choice."

Moving along the corridor, shadows seemed to move along with us, as if of their own accord. Spiders appeared in the corners, scurrying along before vanishing, and at one point we passed a mirror that didn't show our reflections at all, but images of what I suppose our souls were like. Mine, to my relief was gleaming a rosy gold, with only small spots of gray around the edges. Those could be polished away, I figured, with some help from my team.

After continuing past several of these corridors,

we reached a room that was exactly what I'd imagined a witch's room would look like. Well, maybe not real witches, but fairy tale versions. I'm talking skulls, caldrons, all that bullshit you know the 'real witches' don't actually touch. In a world where fairy tales are real, though, the idea of real witches gets a bit muddy.

"It's in here?" I asked, glancing around and hoping to be the first to spot it.

"I wish," she said. "What we will find here is a locator spell, but even for that we'll need something belonging to the Golden Goose."

"Like a feather?" a witch asked with a heavy New Orleans accent. She stepped out from the far corner, where a shorter secret entrance emerged. This witch was short, with dark skin that was even darker in most places because of tattoos in the shapes of birds. Her purple robes were pulled around her tight, showing off cleavage that didn't quite fit on such a petite frame. "It was stolen, unfortunately."

"Toewi, Queen of Crows, what're you doing here?" Mirna asked, hands up, ready to cast a spell. Now I understood the tattoos, though wasn't familiar with the tale of any queen of crows.

"Same as you," Toewi said, "I'd thought at first. Then I noticed your company, and figured hiding out, making an escape... wasn't enough. Whatever this is," she indicated us, making a circle with her finger in the air, "I want in."

"That's a conversation for another time," Elisa said.

"Either way, regarding this house? I want out."

"That can be accommodated," Hekate interjected. "And actually, you can be of some assistance. Tracking spell, and be quick about it."

"There was a feather here, once, but it's gone. We need to find out where it is now."

Toewi laughed.

"Something funny?" Red asked.

"Ironic, considering I'd heard about your recent visit overseas to a mutual friend's house." Toewi had a glimmer in her eyes as she turned to Hekate. "Didn't think anyone was paying attention to your comings and goings, did you?"

Hekate glared, then laughed. "Oh, you've got to be kidding me."

"What?"

"Turns out we don't even need a tracking spell." Hekate glanced over at our new friend, sharing a knowing look. "We're going to have to go back to visit an old friend. Ali Baba."

"Bingo," Toewi said. "He stole it not so long ago, apparently in an attempt to find the Golden Goose herself."

"Great," Sharon growled.

"So, what?" Pucky asked. "We open a portal, go back and ask for it?"

"Yes," Mirna replied, nodding to the door. "But they won't work in the house until we get the wards off. For now, we'd best be moving."

"And why do we need her?" Mirna said, eyeing Toewi with contempt.

"I can open the portal, but we're going to want to just send one of us through, the rest staying here, ready to make a break for it."

"One of us?" I asked.

Elisa nodded. "That makes sense. We all show up there, we're bound to trip alarms, or scare the hell out of him if he's hanging around like last time."

"I guess that'll be me, then."

Nobody argued.

"And why we need Toewi," Hekate said to Mirna, "is because nobody knows the wards here better than her. Seeing as I'd imagine we already triggered the signaling wards or she wouldn't be here—"

"Correct," Toewi said, grinning wide.

"—I'd say we need to get new ones up, ASAP, along with cloaking and whatever else we can to keep ourselves from being a target, at least until Jack can return with the feather."

"There you have it," Toewi said, then nodded to

me. "But you had better get going, because we're only going to be able to hold it for so long."

My glance at Hekate told her I was ready, so she set up the portal. Having the witches on our side made all the difference. With a 'here goes everything' glance to my team and then Chris, I stepped through at the same moment as an explosion sounded, screams erupting from somewhere, and all of it cut out as chanting sounded louder, closer… then gone.

I found myself back in Ali Baba's living room, with the knowledge that the others were under attack. I had to find that feather, and find it fast.

li Baba's living room, though clearly the same room we'd visited before, was changed beyond all recognition since last time I'd been there. For one, while before it had looked like a normal room but cluttered with odd artifacts, now it was empty except for several trip wires and clear traps set up for the defensive.

"Ali Baba, please," I started, knowing taking a shot here wouldn't be good for me or the future of humanity. "I only have one request, something that…"

The wall suddenly exploded, turning into a massive mouth that came at me, accompanied by a flight of arrows and waves of magic. Whatever this man was expecting, I hoped he hadn't set this up for me. My only chance of escape here was the window behind me, as the expanding wall that had come to life had already covered the portal.

So I thrust myself backwards, runes lighting up on my skin as I relied on their power to push me through. The last thing I needed was to slam against the glass and bounce back to be eaten by that wall. Luckily, the glass shattered and I went crashing through, and started to fall.

Double luckily, I had a flying lion that burst forth from my chest, so that mid-fall I was able to grab hold and go soaring out over the streets lined with yellow-brick red-roofed houses.

"I'm glad you're with me," I shouted to the lion, as we swept around to see the rest of the wall follow in the pattern of the window, exploding outward as if a bomb had gone off.

Holy hell, if my team had come with me, I imagined half of them might be dead at this point. As for Ali Baba, I had no idea where to start.

As fate would have it though, more attacks came my way a second later and provided me with more answers than I imagined my attackers would've meant to give up. For example, if they had simply left me to fly off, I never would've had the idea that the next building over housed the enemies who'd set the trap, or that Ali Baba wasn't himself behind it.

I dove down on my flying lion, easily avoiding

crossbow bolts and even a barrage of bullets, and my mind starting to fill in the blanks. The enemy had some reason to want him, right? Had they been waiting to kill him, and I'd foiled it?

Only way to find out would be to get one of them alive. I reminded myself that this had to be quick so that I could get back in time to help my team in the fight back at the witches' mansion.

"Can you get me in there?" I asked Roar, and he roared in response, diving toward one of the balconies below where the attacks were coming from.

We stormed through, twisting and weaving, and then he dove and I jumped, landing on the balcony and slamming through the glass door. Yeah, that hurt, but my tattoos activated and gave me the boosts I needed. No recovery required, I was in and charging up the stairs. The first of the goons met me there, trying to shoot at me. I threw up my forearm so my shield formed, deflecting the shots and making me feel very much like Captain America, but then I was leaping up and maiming them with my blade, each strike making it glow more with blue energy, until the moment I charged into the room above and was able to slam it down and send a shock wave through a group of them.

"Who the fuck are you?" a woman shouted in a thick accent, standing and aiming a pistol at me.

That threw me for a loop, but I aimed my sword back at her, ready to bring up my shield. "I'm the Protector. Who the fuck are you?"

"Shit, this isn't even them," she hissed to the bloodied guy pushing himself up next to her.

"Son?" a shout came from the back room, and then a thud.

I recognized that voice, so charged back, holding up my forearm and shield to block the shots as the woman fired on me. Flying through the door, I found two guards turning from Ali Baba, who was latched to a chair with a glowing chain—the type that, I imagined, stifled any sort of magic or charms he might have otherwise used to escape.

"Ali Baba," I said, sliding in to take out the first and hoping my glamour was gone. "It's me. Jack."

The guard was—I had to figure—on the side of evil here. It was the only way I could think about the fact that I'd just sliced his gut open. I'd been hoping to go for some fancy move that would knock them unconscious, but honestly didn't know much about that. What I knew was that all my upgrading in the mists of the Fae World had made me fast and strong. My next move was an attempt to use that to my advantage, kicking out the second guard's legs and slamming in the back of the head with the pummel of my sword.

It cracked against his skull and he fell, but cursed loudly, stumbling as he tried to stand again. So much for that idea. When I saw a gun, I knew it was either me or him, so removed head from body in an awesome display of instinct taking over.

No prana or ichor. No leveling up.

Just blood.

A shiver ran up my spine watching it seep out like that,

"Damn, boy…" Ali Baba said, then shouted to look out behind me.

I spun, shield up and met the woman from before with my sword in her gut. Pushing her back, I thought I was going to puke.

"What is this?" Ali Baba asked. "You're here to save me?"

Holding up a hand, I worked to keep the bile down, to not think about the blood around me and on my sword, likely on my clothes. The metallic smell of the blood made it worse.

"Better move fast." Ali Baba shifted his chair around. "Magical binds. Cut me loose, so I can help you."

Finally pulling myself together, I did so, then helped him to his feet. He was the old man we'd met before, but looked to have aged considerably more, long gray eyebrows hanging over the sides of his face, almost touching his white beard.

"It wasn't so long ago we met," I said, perplexed. "How…?"

He grunted, shaking his head. "Magic kept me young, but they raided the place, took it all."

"All?" I felt my stomach churning. "And… this?"

"Bait. Not for you, though—for my son. Seems he's pissed someone off, even before this little war started."

"It's not little," I countered. "And I need your help —I need a feather. A golden feather."

His eyebrows shot up. "Even if you had it, it won't do you any good. Only works on spirits, but this one's a dud."

"Except we're using it for a different purpose."

"You… have a witch?" He laughed. "A tracking spell, with the hopes of finding the real golden goose? You're mad."

"Well, they can't have gotten far with it, right?" I glanced around. "Based on this setup, it might even still be nearby."

He nodded. "Top floor—penthouse. They have a small army, so I don't know how you expect to get up there."

"I have a lion," I replied with a wink, and then

picked up the guards' pistols. "Any idea what we're dealing with up there?"

Ali Baba was still watching me, skeptically. "Yeah, enough to take me down. Though to be fair, I was in the middle of a bath."

"At least they gave you clothes before tying you up."

He nodded in conceit. "Party that did it, their leader—you might know him as the Dragon of the North."

"Doesn't ring a bell," I admitted.

He shrugged. "Not one of the more popular stories in the States, but suffice it to say he's not someone to easily dismiss." A pounding sounded, then doors opening and shouting followed. "And he's definitely the type to be sending troops down to check on this situation, so…"

"Got it, move. Come on."

I took off running for the window, shooting it this time to avoid hurting myself as much when I went crashing through. Shouts of "What the fuck?" came from behind, but before any of the goons had a chance to make a move, Ali Baba and I were out through the window.

He screamed, turning to me in panic as we started to fall, but I reached out my hand and caught him by the forearm. Just then, Roar came swinging around. I landed on the lion and pulled Ali Baba around behind me, and then we were up, soaring past the stupid faces of the goons, up and up until we were level with the penthouse. Here we could see the windows that led in, along with a large balcony with a hot tub.

A guard was fucking a woman in the hot tub, both startled to see us land and hop off Roar.

"They're all bad people?" I asked.

Ali Baba tilted his head, and said, "They're all people. Some have children."

"Fuck." I held up my new pistol, nodding toward the building. "You two, go find your master, tell him I'm here for a golden feather."

They scampered off. The woman slipped as she went, the man not even bothering to turn back to help her up.

"Would've been easier if you just let me kill them," I said.

"I didn't say you couldn't, just pointed out a fact." He eyed me. "You know, for the Protector, you sure think about things a bit too much."

I scoffed, starting to walk toward the building and calling after the man, "Tell them, as long as they don't shoot at or attack us, they won't die. None of the people in there need to die today, but they better leave, pronto."

The man paused at the door, looked back, and then gestured for the woman to hurry.

"You know they'll come out shooting," Ali Baba said.

"And then I won't feel bad about killing them," I replied, adrenaline taking over so that I genuinely wasn't worried. All I could think of at the moment was getting that damn feather and returning to my team as fast as possible. "Where do you think it would be?"

He frowned, ran a hand along his beard, and then said, "Most of it, probably in the main room of the suite. Maybe they've started carting some of it out, but I had a lot of good stuff. They're probably still trying to inventory it."

"And… how much can you leave behind?"

He frowned. "I'm not leaving it in their hands."

"I don't see how you have much of a choice. We're going to get what we can, including that feather, and then get out of here as fast as possible. If I can get away with as few deaths as possible, that would be great."

He clucked his tongue, breathed heavily. "Then we blow it."

"As in…?"

"I'll get what I need, then light a fuse. I have

plenty of magic that will result in an explosion. But you see two gold wrist cuffs, you give them to me."

I frowned, nodded, and said, "Here goes," indicating the line of men and women now visible through the window, guns aimed at us. "Stay behind me."

He chuckled, kneeling and scratching with something on the cement under our feet. "Don't you worry about me."

I knelt and held up my forearm as the glass shattered, bullets coming in our direction. Many of them hit my shield, but the majority seemed to hit some sort of wind tunnel and be swept aside, and into the cement behind us, so that the area around the hot tub was peppered.

A glance over revealed Ali Baba grinning, the lines he'd drawn in the ground glowing. Seeing this, and realizing that's where the change in direction of the bullets came from, I completely understood how lucky the enemy had been to catch him in the bath.

The first round of shots stopped, the enemy staring in confusion, and I charged, returning fire with the pistol and, when I was close enough, hitting them with a group strike from my sword. Already a handful or more were down, Ali Baba taking up the rear and pausing to scratch two new marks in the walls as he passed. More guards turned on us, but started firing wildly. I glanced back and stifled a laugh—whatever he'd just done must've been some sort of illusion ward, because it looked like there were fifty of us charging in there.

"We're being overrun!" one of the men said into his comms, a moment before my sword cut him open. I spun and shot another who was about to shoot in Ali Baba's direction, and the old man gave me a nod of gratitude.

"Make for the stash," I said, and Ali Baba nodded, leaving me to take down three more guards on my way.

I did my thing with them and was halfway to the door he'd just opened, when he leaped back and a burst of flames exploded outward. Walls caught fire, corpses of fallen goons catching too, while Ali Baba rolled to put out a flame on his sleeve and then was quickly sketching more wards into the wall at his side.

My advance had come to a stop just short of the range of the fire, and now I wasn't so sure I wanted to keep going. There had to be another way about this.

A heavy step sounded, a moment later this massive beast of a woman stepping through the doorway. While mostly human in her look, she wore flowing robes over her scaled, muscular body, and had the face of a yellow dragon.

Huh, the Dragon of the North was female. There was no doubt this was her. I don't know why I thought otherwise, and wondered if Ali Baba had referred to her as a he.

When her eyes landed on me, she cocked her head, knelt, and prepared for another attack. Since something about the wards were letting Ali Baba sneak behind her in that moment, I figured me taking the attack, as long as I could survive it, made a lot of sense. At least until he could get what he needed.

But first, I thought I'd try another tactic.

"The legendary Dragon of the North," I said, sounding very impressed.

She eyed me, closed her mouth, and then waited.

"I mean, to finally meet you in person, oh great Dragon. This is an honor." I bowed, holding my sword out to the side as if it were more of a ceremonial piece. Meanwhile, flames rose up along the walls of the room, but I had to try and ignore that little fact.

"Protector," she said in a raspy voice, smoke trailing out from her nostrils. "Will it stink when you burn? Being full of shit, and all."

I laughed. "It's not every day a sexy, beautiful

fairy tale such as yourself has a sense of humor to boot."

This time she laughed—a laugh that brought a small burst of flame. "Now you're mocking me?"

"Not mocking. Hell, do you know how many ways I'd bend you backwards?"

"Isn't there only one way to bend backwards?"

"See," I said, stepping forward, putting on my best cool-guy look. It was a stretch, but I was feeling pretty confident with how buff I'd gotten lately. "That shows you how much you have to learn, and I'm here to teach you."

Maybe it was my imagination, but I could've sworn her cheeks had turned orange—was she blushing?

With a sigh, she shook her head. "A shame I have to kill you, instead."

"You're… positive?"

She looked me up and down, her reptilian tongue darting out briefly, and then she nodded. "Maybe I'll at least eat your flesh afterward. We can still join as one, just not in the way you had in mind."

At that moment, I saw Ali Baba behind her give me a wave, two gold bracers on his wrists. It was time. Also, she'd just grossed me out.

"I hate to be a party pooper, but fuck that," I said, and then charged. As her flames burst forth, I knew the shield wouldn't be enough so pulled on another strength—my Tempest powers. The glass was down, water out there from the hot tub, and I thrust, pulling on it with everything I had.

Flames were inches from my face by the time the water hit, flooding over her and sending the dragon sputtering backwards while I slid down, going across the ground and rolling. When I came up swinging, she spun and knocked me down with her wings. I sliced, blade hitting scales and leaving her unharmed.

She opened her mouth to breathe flames again, but none came. Only a gargling, choking sound.

"We got what we came for," Ali Baba shouted, darting insanely fast past me and dragging me along the way. How he was moving like that was beyond me, but he had the feather in his free hand. A long, beautiful golden feather.

He was right, there was no point risking our lives to kill this dragon lady right then, not if we could escape with what we needed. Flee the battle to win the war.

"Rain check, then?" she called out after me, and I paused at the edge of the roof.

"For which? The eating me part, or a good fuck?" I shouted back.

She tilted her head. "I still don't see why we can't do both."

"You've got issues," I yelled, as I leaped, calling for my lion. A moment later, Ali Baba and I were back on Roar, soaring toward Ali's apartment. A screech sounded above and I turned to see the dragon growing in size, flapping her wings, and moving in pursuit.

"Fuck me," I muttered, and leaned forward, close to Roar, watching with anticipation as we closed on the open wall, the portal beyond.

The dragon soared overhead, Ali Baba shouting that we needed to hurry, and then we were in, Roar collapsing into my chest, and the two of us tumbling toward the portal. Only, it was closing!

I leaped, triggering all sorts of traps as I threw myself at the portal but knew I wasn't going to make it. Ali Baba was suddenly at my side, purple smoke surrounding us as we were hurtled through the portal and came tumbling out the other side.

As soon as we were through, I saw why the portal was closing. Hekate was on her side, holding her head. The walls beside us had been blasted away, and the rest of my team was in the courtyard in the heat of battle.

17

**W**e're here, close it!" I shouted, running to make sure Hekate was okay.

She rolled over, saw me and the gold feather, and nodded. The portal faded with a puff of smoke, I imagined from fire on the other side.

"Get out there, I'll be fine," she said. "Just took a bit of a beating there."

"Hekate," Ali Baba said, giving her a brief nod, joining me to make our way to the fight below. From what I could see—illusions gone and all—a Pucky was doing a good job holding off the enemy with her massive rifle, and Elisa made shields of white light when needed.

"Care to explain your little magic display back there?" I asked as we ran.

Ali Baba grinned, holding up his arms and the gold. "Got these a while back—gives me the power of being a genie, basically, as long as I wear them. Only problem, they're draining. Wear them too long, and I risk actually becoming one."

"Damn." I glanced over, glad I wasn't relying on powers with such a risk. "And your son? The trap?"

He grimaced, but shook his head. "No, he wouldn't go back. He's smart enough to know that, ever since that wife of his saved my ass back in the day, I've learned to fend for myself. There's not a situation I can't get out of."

"With my help," I reminded him.

"And you only got out of there with mine," he replied with a wink.

"Touché."

We reached a point where he could use his genie power to lower me down. While I could've done it with Roar, this was faster and I hadn't relied on Roar enough to know if there was any sort of price for calling on him too often, so figured letting him rest wouldn't be the worst idea.

Hekate followed a moment later, reaching out and saying, "The feather. I'll get the tracking spell going."

"Roger that," I replied, trying to sound formal but earning a laugh from her.

"Here in Witch World, we prefer 'fuck yeah,' or 'here you go, dipshit.'"

I chuckled, trying to figure out a good point to interject myself into the fight. "What're we dealing with, exactly?"

"Persephone, for one," Hekate said, indicating a line of witches, one tall and floating, swirling with a tornado of darkness forming. "The rest of the witches, at least any that weren't out on the front lines."

"And I see an old enemy," Ali Baba grunted, suddenly taking off and clashing with a man who'd been about to attack Red.

"Looks like he found the Mouse King," Hekate said, cringing. She turned to cast a spell of silvery blast that sent two incoming witches to the ground.

I circled up against a man with a wand that kept sending out green sparks my way, but my shield handled them well enough. When I ended him with my sword, a red ball of ichor flew over.

Quickly checking to see what skills I could add, I saw one that allowed me to summon my sword if it had fallen away. While I had been able to in the water with Arthur, that had been because of the water. Now, anywhere, anyhow, if I could get that skill. It could come in very handy, and since I didn't have much time to analyze the various paths, decided that worked. I applied the ichor and got the upgrade.

More witches and gods were coming our way, some flying, and I realized this wasn't the time for Roar to be resting. I called him out and he soared up, immediately swooping down again and tackling a man with wild, silvery hair, so that he slammed into the ground while Roar took on what looked like a flying rat as large as himself.

I rose up and brought my sword down to cleave the man's head in two, then was sent flying sideways by a spell from a woman with lizard features. My team was fighting all around me, Red at my side a second later to help me back up and counter the next spell before it hit me. Elisa was busy throwing up shields of light to keep Persephone's attacks off of us. The goddess would dart around in bursts of darkness, sending attack after attack at us, none of what we sent her way landing.

With this force against ours, it was clear we needed to get out of there if we didn't want to get pinned down in a long battle.

"This way," Red shouted, pulling me toward Hekate. We found three witches trying to take her down with binding and freezing spells, but Red took out two with quick dashing movements and slicing open their necks, while I sent a blast from my sword that took the next one out of commission.

Soon we had the others from our team, huddled up while Elisa made shields and Hekate sent counter spells.

"What do we need to get out of here?" Pucky shouted over the chaos.

"We've got the feather and I've started the first steps of the locator spell, but it takes time." Hekate took Chris's arm in hers, looking over the group. "So... next step is finding Goldilocks, then?"

"I know exactly where she is," Red said. "But it's not going to be fun."

"Why?" I asked.

"Last I heard—and this wasn't so long ago—she's heavy in the underground network. Those neutrals who don't want to be messed with."

"That sounds like a *lot* of fun," I countered with a chuckle.

She arched an eyebrow, shook her head, and waited while Hekate made the portal per her instructions.

As we entered the portal, I chanced a glance back and was amazed at what I saw. Not only nearby, but as far as I could see there were what looked like Pyramids descending toward the ground—upside-down pyramids. In some places it was more like pagodas, but no matter the shape they all shared the fact that they were descending, light blaring and flashing between them. No, not descending, I realized. Becoming visible.

"Only visible to us," Hekate said, seeing the look on my face. "Because we have this now." She held up the golden feather, and I got it.

The Golden Goose was on one of those crazy sky pyramids. Where, I imagined, the gods were coming from. First, we were going after Goldilocks, yes, but then our mission would be taking us up there, and that was terrifying.

18

While crazy pyramids of gods and Legends were making their assault on the world above, we were, apparently, moving into the underbelly of some city. Hekate took us via portal to an underground network of caves and old military tunnels in the mountains of Montana.

"Not many people know about this place," Hekate explained, "because the military abandoned it and ordered it closed quite a while back."

"Since then it's been the rumored hideout of the all the black-market handlers, thugs, and all manner of assholes that refuse to side with the Legends or Myths," Red explained. "But since you know about it, I'd say it tends more toward the side of Legends."

Hekate grunted in the affirmative.

The current tunnel had bunks built into the sides, several strange fairy tale characters watching us with furrowed brows. One had little deer horns growing form his head, another a face that was somewhere between human and dragon—it was almost hot, in a weird, reptilian sort of way. I had to smile at that thought, humored by how far I'd come since becoming part of this world. Sure, I'd enjoyed such stories as *Monster Musume*, but never actually been able to see myself with any sort of odd creature. Since getting involved with Pucky, her horns had kind of acted as a gateway drug for me, opening my mind to all manner of oddities.

We left the main tunnel to climb down a ladder and find ourselves in what looked like an old bunker, but had the smell of a sewer. It was hot down there, making the stench even worse. At the far end, a door opened and about half a dozen thugs entered. Some carried batons, others baseball bats, crowbars, and one even had a large shotgun over his shoulder.

"Word is you've gone over," the one with the shotgun said.

"Who's he talking to?" I asked, but Hekate stepped ahead of us, motioning for us to stay put.

"That's what they're saying?" Hekate asked. "Well, they're fucking right. The line has been drawn, and it's time everyone here chose a side."

"Fuck that." The guy lowered the shotgun our way.

"Keep pointing that thing at me," Red said, "and you won't see tomorrow."

The man's eyes went to her and he hesitated, lifting the shotgun. "Fucking Red Riding Hood?" His eyes kept moving as we drew closer, and he froze, blinking. "What the fuck kind of group have you all put together? This is some *Suicide Squad* shit going on, or what?"

"Wait, from the comics, or the movie?" I asked, ignoring the confused looks from around me.

He chuckled. "Fucked if I know what you're talking about—there was a movie? Nah, I mean from the comics."

"Ah, man, you missed a damn-good Harley Quinn, but…" I stopped there, not wanting to trash talk the movie, and realizing everyone was still staring at me. "What, I mean—shared interests, right? It's a good thing."

A tense moment was broken by the man chuckling. "Who the fuck's this kid?"

"Jack," I answered. "New Protector."

His buddies scoffed and laughed, but stopped at a look from him.

"That right?" He stepped closer, eyeing me, then turning to Red. "Sorry about before. Didn't realize",

and, turning back to me, he thrust out a hand, "welcome to the fucking tunnels, Protector." After we
shook hands, he turned to Hekate. "I'm not saying
we're taking sides, yet, but I'll say this—we aren't
standing in your way."

"Boss—" one started, but shut his mouth when
the guy turned his way.

"We're not stupid enough to do that," the
apparent boss said. "Plus, I like the new kid."

The others made confused faces, but stepped
aside when he motioned them to.

"Goldi in there?" Red asked.

The man flinched at that, but nodded. "Fuck, this
better be important. She'll have my balls if you're
going in there to… I don't know, do anything she
doesn't like."

"We mean to hire her," Hekate said.

This made all of their expressions change to
curiosity.

"You manage that," the boss said, "we know
which team we'll be on."

"And we'll hold you to it," Red replied as we
walked past them and through the doorway.

"I kinda like him," I admitted.

"If you knew the shit he's pulled over the years,
you might not," Hekate said, but then turned to

Chris and frowned. "Then again, Chris forgave me my mis-deeds."

Chris shrugged. "Killing, burning... all that—it was a different you."

I turned so they wouldn't see my disapproval. At least with Sharon, her past had been influenced by shadow magic, which I completely understood. As far as I knew with Hekate and these goons, that wasn't the case.

We kept pushing on, checking various hideouts, going through old war rooms and whatnot that had been turned into living quarters. Not a sign of her, nor much else. It was practically a ghost town. Or, ghost tunnel place.

"Why so empty?" I asked.

"I had a hunch it would be this way," Hekate said. "Cleared out. Taken down by the agents or off to fight in the war now raging between Myths and Legends."

"What if she's not here?" I asked. "Maybe she went off to fight, joined in..."

"Then we'd be fucked," Red said. "More than likely, she'd be on the other side."

"And you think she'll help us?"

Red glanced my way, then shook her head. "No. Not on her own, but with a bit of persuading."

"Meaning what, exactly?" Pucky asked.

"We find leverage."

Elisa turned, eyes narrowed, then suddenly glanced around. "Not them...."

I was as confused as Pucky and, it seemed, Sharon, but an answer came a moment later when Pucky kicked open a door and charged in, blade out and ready. Okay, maybe not the answer—but a start to an answer.

We followed her, not sure what to expect.

"RAHHH!" a roar came, then a large form charging through and slamming into Chris. When the man turned, he was transforming into a bear! Two more men were following behind, transforming as they came.

"Fuck this," Sharon said, going full wolf and dwarfing them as she went for the two newcomers. Hekate and the other witches had already started dealing with the first, and I was surprised to see Chris bust out a spell of his own as flames erupted from his fingers, catching on the bear.

I didn't want to release Roar underground, so went for my sword instead. Our other teammates were faster than me to act though, with Red and her cloak darting forward, Elisa thrusting blinding light at the enemy and then boosts on us. The witches and Chris doing their part.

"Don't kill them!" Elisa shouted as we made

impact, and I turned to see Hekate actually putting out the fire on the first bear.

"What?" I shouted, confused.

"These are her bears—we kill them, she's definitely not going to help us."

"Fuck!" Red shouted back, darting and kicking to sweep out a bear's legs, while seconds before she'd been ready to knife the bastard.

The still standing one roared and lunged for Pucky, who teleported past it and caught it with a swift kick in the ass. Still, it managed to get Red and slam her against the wall. Goldi or not, I wasn't about to let the bear hurt Red, so I prepared to slice the beast.

"I'm not getting involved," a voice said, and everyone froze.

We spun around to see a woman with a look of a dark-haired Madonna stepping out of the shadows. As much as they'd said her name came from her ability with locks and not her hair as the legends claimed, I found it humorous that she was wearing bracelets of interlocked gold chains.

"Just one job," Red said, pushing the bear off of her, standing tall as if the fight had never happened. "The Golden Goose."

Goldi scoffed. "You're out of your damn mind. Nobody can get to it, nobody—"

Ali Baba held up the golden feather, and Hekate waved her hand, causing golden light to swirl above it, leading off to our left.

"Shit, you…" Goldi stepped forward, reaching for the feather.

"Not so fast," Red said, knife closer to the bear's throat.

Ali Baba moved his hands and the feather was gone. A simple sleight of hand, definitely more trick than magic, but still, impressive.

"Let him go, bitch," Goldi said. "You should've known the moment you showed me the locator spell, I'd be in."

"Had to have insurance," Red said, pushing the bear away.

"Wait, so… she's in?" I asked.

Goldi turned my way. "Who's the new boy?"

"Man," I corrected her.

"Protector," Red corrected me.

I nodded, standing tall.

"No shit?" Goldi smiled, seductively. "He claimed yet?"

"We're with him," Pucky said, horns starting to glow as she stepped toward Goldi. "So back the fuck off."

Goldi held up her hands and laughed. "You ever

get bored of them and wanna become a fourth bear, let me know."

"Fourth...?" I said, then looked at her three bears, realizing they had some sort of golden chains around their necks that matched her bracelets. "They're your slaves?"

"Willing," Goldi countered, a bit too fast. "They can leave whenever they want to. But as long as they're with me, they do what the fuck I say, when I say."

"Like a Reverse Harem?" Chris asked.

She turned to him now. "Fuck you."

"What'd I say?"

"I think it's the way you said it," I offered, really having no idea.

"No," Goldi motioned to one of the bears. "Are you part of a harem?"

He scrunched his nose, then chuckled. "Sure am."

"There you go," Goldi turned back to me, then Chris, as if she'd just proven her case. "Did I have to say 'reverse' in there? No, don't be stupid."

"It works with books," Chris mumbled.

"Genre shit," she replied. "Not real fucking life. Don't try to label my lovers ever again. You, you're not invited. No bear invite for you."

Chris opened his mouth as if about to reply, but a glance from Mirna got him to shut up.

Without another look our way, Goldi turned back to Red and said, "I'm doing this for me, to be clear, but when this is over, we're square. Good?"

"Agreed," Red said, ignoring the curious glances her way. She turned to Hekate and nodded. "Make it happen."

"Oh, well…" Hekate frowned. "You do realize I can't open a portal to the pyramids?"

"What?"

"Up there—I can't. It's impossible."

"So how do we do it?" Elisa asked.

Hekate and Mirna shared a look. "Those of us who can fly…. Fly."

We all looked around, realizing this wasn't going to let all of us go.

"Good fucking plan," Goldi said.

"That mean… who, exactly?" Sharon asked, eyes roaming over all of us.

"I'm good at falling," Red said.

"She's real good at going down," Pucky added. "Sorry, couldn't help it. I'm—me too, I'm also good at that. Does saying so make my joke go away, or make it worse?"

"Worse," Elisa said, shaking her head. "Honestly, I think I can get up there with the help of my brother's power, but barely. Hekate?"

"I can fly, but just me," Hekate replied.

Goldi had her arms folded, shaking her head, clearly about to lose confidence in the plan. With that in mind, I had an idea.

"Roar."

Everyone turned back at me. One of the bears arched an eyebrow, then smiled and said, "Roar back, big guy."

"Sorry, I mean—my lion. I call him Roar."

"Lions don't fly," Goldi countered.

I chuckled. "Mine does."

"And might be able to carry one more," Elisa said. "We'll need what we can get—so looks like it'll be you and Goldi on the lion, Hekate to keep the tracking spell going, and me... to kick ass when necessary."

"That'll have to do," Goldi said, eyes roaming over me.

"Keep your hands off of him, or when you get back you'll answer to me," Pucky said, glaring at Goldi.

"I wouldn't let her," I said.

"It's not you I'm worried about."

Goldi frowned, then sighed. "I promise not to try and sneak any fondling sessions with your boy while we're up there saving the world."

I coughed, trying to get that image out of my head real fast. We all turned, moving outside and preparing to make for the pyramid that the golden light was pointing to—one out of our current line of sight.

"Wait here, or meet back at the mansion?" Red asked.

"My mansion," Elisa replied. "Mirna can get you there, and we'll go with Hekate."

Chris grinned wide. "I miss that place."

"Oh, no." Elisa cocked her head, then added, "Red, Pucky, show them the guest room and burn the sheets when they're done."

Mirna laughed, and shrugged. "Yeah, if we have down time, we're probably going to get nasty. It's just a fact of life."

At least it was good to know we weren't the only ones like that.

Without further ado, Hekate held out her hand and made a broom appear from the thin air while Elisa braced herself, about to call on her brothers's power to propel her.

"On you," Elisa said to me.

I put my hand on my chest, nodding for Goldi to join me, then called on my lion. He burst out, wings spread wide and nearly knocking over one of Goldi's bears. He roared, looked around, and then settled his gaze on me. As if knowing my thoughts, he lowered himself so that I could climb on and pull Goldi up behind me.

"Watch those hands," Pucky growled.

Goldi was behind me, but I imagine she made some sort of lewd gesture because a moment later Pucky was charging for her and Red had to step in to break it up.

"Pucky, dear," I said, hand caressing the lion's neck to show him we were ready. "If I feel her hands anywhere they don't belong, I promise to chop them off myself. We'll send them down in a nice little package, bow tie and all."

"Aw, that's so sweet," Pucky said, blowing me a kiss.

"I don't think it's sweet at all," Goldi hissed, and then we were in the air with a mighty leap from Roar, Elisa bursting up in an explosion of white light a moment later, and then Hekate appeared on her broom.

Next stop: crazy pyramid home of some god or whatever the hell it was.

19

I had to imagine it was a spell from Hekate or one of the others that allowed us to reach the pyramid without being attacked. Whatever the reason, I was relieved to find that we were flying up and into an opening, none of the gods there noticing.

"Don't move, and they won't," a voice said, and I glanced around to see that Goldi was looking pointedly at each of us in turn. So it had actually been her, and even now we were cloaked. There was more to her than simply picking locks.

We were passing all manner of so-called gods, some with their togas and animal forms from Greek mythology, others with colorful African clothes, one even holding an actual lightning bolt that sizzled in his hand.

One of the gods started to turn our way, but Goldi motioned back and we floated off from the main area and into a passage. From there we were able to see that god step forward, look around, and then turn away again.

"Figures Loki would be the one to almost see us," Goldi said with a grin.

"She's always had a crush on him," Elisa whispered my way. "But won't ever admit it."

"Still won't," Goldi whispered back, then turned to Hekate. "You're up."

Hekate nodded, taking the golden feather and waving a hand over it. Her eyes turned to gold, and she pointed. "This way."

As we kept going, we passed rooms full of shifting darkness, and on the third one I realized they were rooms full of Shades. At least once I saw some taller than should've been possible, and recognized one of the tall, colossus looking mother fuckers I had thought I'd seen back in the mists of the Fae world.

"They're collecting them," I said, turning to see that Goldi only gave me a 'who cares' look. It was easy to forget she wasn't exactly on our side.

"What you should care about," she hissed as we moved on, "is that you're on what's basically a ship of gods, or at least very powerful fairy tales who will gladly tear you to shreds if they find us."

"Tear *us* to shreds," I corrected her.

She winked. "We'll see."

I didn't want to know what she meant by that, and turned back to Elisa, wishing more of my immediate team had been able to join us. At least I had Roar, if needed.

"Don't worry, it won't come to that," Elisa said, stepping up to walk at my side, so that Goldi led the way with Hekate checking our rear.

"You'd save me?" I asked with a chuckle.

She stared, deadpan. "Yes. Know this, you're our Protector, and more and more you've grown into that role—and done your job well. But I'd die before seeing any harm come to you."

"Doesn't that defeat the purpose?" Goldi said, voice low like ours to avoid detection. "I mean, you have a Protector, he's supposed to do the protecting."

"Actually, his job is to protect on a larger scale. So you could say that if he allowed me to sacrifice myself so that he could live, he'd be making the right move."

"And I'll say right now, if that ever happens you can count on me walking," I protested.

"Don't say that," Elisa put a hand on my arm. "You mustn't."

"Just—don't let it come to that."

She nodded, looking troubled, but then shook her head. "Listen, we don't have to worry about it, as long as we win. So let's win."

"You all always talk like this?" Hekate asked, glaring and looking like she was going to be sick. "Fuck."

"What, you and Chris haven't moved on to holding hands yet?" I asked with a grin, mostly trying to forget the situation we were in. Moving up a set of stairs, eerie gold lines along the walls glowed, at times pulsating in a way that made me feel even more uncomfortable.

Hekate hadn't stopped glaring, but there was a hint of a smile at the corner of her mouth.

"Ah, she's got it bad," Elisa said with a chuckle.

"Got what?" Hekate asked.

"You're in love."

Hekate actually stopped at that. "Don't be stupid."

"Can we apply that to all of you?" Goldi said, motioning to a passage to her right. "We have me here for a reason, but that won't mean shit if we don't find out where they're keeping it. So, tracker?"

"We're on the right path," Hekate said, indicating the way we were going. "But there at the next landing up, it looks like we turn right,."

"And you all were so certain you'd need my skills, why?"

"You ever met a god who didn't keep the goods locked away?" Elisa asked.

Goldi frowned, then shrugged and kept going.

Sure enough, we turned right when directed, and then came to an intricate system of light we had seen before. The blocks shimmered with a faint light. Goldi glanced at Hekate, who nodded and pointed ahead.

"It's a pattern," Goldi said, analyzing it all with a finger at the side of her chin. "And if the spell is saying this is the way, then this is our path."

Staring at the lights, trying to find any rhyme or reason to them, I frowned. "How is this a pattern?"

Goldi put a finger to the side of her head, turned it, and said, "You need to have a screw or two loose to be on my level, Mr."

I chuckled. "I'll keep that in mind."

"Maybe I screw you a bit and help speed along the process? Or… would that be unscrewing?"

"How about you keep your vagina in your pants and focus on the task at hand?"

"This is starting to get fun," Hekate said, grinning wide.

"She'll come for your Chris next," Elisa countered.

Hekate frowned at that, then pointed a finger in Goldilocks' chest. "Focus on the puzzle."

Goldi chuckled, gave me a flirtatious glance, and returned to the wall. "No worries, I'm just teasing you all. The bears are more than I can handle anyway. One's too big, one too small, the other just right. But together? Woo-eee, they make the perfect trio."

"Way too much info," I said.

"It helps me figure out puzzles," she insisted. "Talking about dick and whatnot. Really, I don't know, gets the mind focused."

I glanced around, expecting the other two to be as confused by this lady as I was, but Hekate looked very interested, Elisa nodding along.

"What?" Elisa said at my look. "It's true. Sometimes when I'm trying to focus on a spell, I just imagine you—well, not you, exactly, but a painting of you. For some reason that works on a level that lets me separate it on a sexual level, but… seeing you there, nude, in the paint? It gives me this warm feeling right here," she put a hand over her heart, "and, of course, a bit downstairs."

Hekate chuckled. "I don't know what you two are talking about, but I'm going to try it next time. So what, you just talk about a good fuck and, boom, mind focus?"

Goldi nodded, moving along the wall. "Yeah, that's right." She knelt, watching the light form a bit of an "L" shape. "For example, just yesterday I had Papa Bear so deep in me I thought I'd break in half, while stroking—"

"Fuck this," I said, turning and walking away, covering my ears. The last thing I wanted to hear about was her getting fingercuffed or whatever she was about to say. Then a thought hit me and I turned around.

"…his nutsack stretched so far—"

"Hold on," I interrupted, glad she stopped at that point. "What about Mama Bear?"

"That's just what we call Gregor," Goldi said, glaring at me in annoyance for interrupting her flow. "He's kind of a fruit, so… yeah. But he likes the term. Know what else he likes?"

"I'll just… be over here." I turned, trying to ignore the way she started describing how she'd go down on him, and luckily, I didn't hear the following details. Instead, I walked back to the entryway, where I could pull up my screen and check out my stats and leveling, to try and figure out what would be a good goal for the next build, as it were.

It seemed my best use of prana if I got more would be in speed and upgrading my shield and other skills, as having over three-hundred percent strength seemed pretty damn good for the moment. As for skills, there were two that looked especially intriguing which I set my sights on. One would allow me to cancel out others powers nearby, which I could certainly see the value of. The other only worked with situations where water was involved— related to me being a Tempest, and allowed me to create simple illusions of myself to confuse the enemy. A definite plus there that could figure into my grand strategy.

When the time came, I'd focus on getting those two.

Laughter sounded from behind and I strained my ears for signs that the gods had heard, but we seemed to be in luck. I turned back anyway, and returned just as the wall was starting to fold out for us.

"Piece of cake," Goldi said at my look of astonishment. "All about finding the connecting patterns and leading them to the entry point."

I followed her through, slightly more impressed with her ability to use sexual stories to solve puzzles and even wondering if I should try that sometime. The question that bugged me, was whether it actually helped, or whether she had really been messing with us.

It didn't matter though, because we were

through, and into a chamber that led to the left, turning twice as it wound around a section of the pyramid. We eventually found ourselves in a room with a central passage, but it led straight up and had no access points before that.

"Of course," she said, eyeing it. "Most of the gods can fly, I imagine."

We were at another stage of the safety check, then, in that only certain types of beings could progress. It just so happened that we could mostly fly—only, I couldn't make it up a narrow passage like that with Roar out.

"Another sex story to figure it out?" I asked.

Goldi chuckled. "This one's probably a lot simpler. Just need these two to get us up there."

Hekate leaned over, assessing the way. "I could get a spell going to throw you each up there. Who's going first?"

All eyes on me.

"Fuck it." I stepped forward, sliding down the edge and making my way to the center of the room. The others came behind.

"If you don't make it…" Goldi shrugged. "At least I'll know to turn around and get out of here ASAP."

"Funny." I looked up the dark passage above, not liking the look of this one bit. "How do we know there's not a wall waiting to slam into my head?"

"Well," Hekate threw her hand up so a fire ball flew up, disappearing above. "There you go."

"Great." Turning back to Goldi, I frowned. "Don't leave me."

She chuckled. "I've come too far."

I nodded, then realized something. "I still don't know why you're really here?"

"The challenge of it all isn't answer enough for you?"

I shook my head.

"Let's just say… for a bit there, we had a fourth bear on its way. One of these fuckers made it not so. I've heard the Golden Goose's eggs can help in situations like mine."

That hit me, and I nodded in silence. My assumption from what she'd said was that she'd been pregnant, but not only had she lost the child, but was now barren. If the eggs could help, then I'd make sure she got one to the best of my ability.

"Here goes," Hekate said, then thrust her hands up. It was like a gust of wind had taken me and launched me into the air, up and through that opening. My arms held close, I thought at any moment I'd slam into the wall and go falling back.

I'm glad to say, that didn't happen. Instead I came out the other side to land in a room full of sticky weed that tried to eat me… Nah, just joking. That's

Harry Potter stuff—all that was in the room I landed in was a hard-as-fuck floor that hurt like hell when I slammed into it on my side. I was still groaning as Goldi followed, landing on me with a leg between mine—dangerously close to ending my ability to have babies.

She smiled, moved her leg against my crotch, and then caught a fist upside the head.

"What'd I say about backing off?" Elisa said, standing there and massaging the fist she'd just hit Goldi with.

"Mother fucker!" Goldi grumbled, recovering but taking a step back, hands up. "A girl can't flirt a bit without getting punched around here?"

"Consider that punch a mercy. Your last warning."

The way Elisa was glaring, her nostrils flaring... I have to admit, it was damn hot. I'd never expected her to be the over-protective or jealous type, but she was proving me wrong and I loved it.

"You've got nothing to worry about from me," I told her, pushing myself up with another groan.

Elisa helped me, and muttered something about knowing that, but still not liking Goldi's attitude. She was interrupted though by Hekate joining us, and laughing at the sight of the bruise forming on Goldi's forehead.

"I always miss the fun." Hekate leaned back against the opening we'd come through. An action that resulted in a shrill sound that seemed to echo throughout the pyramid.

"Shit," Goldi said, turning to Hekate and frowning. "What'd you do?"

Hekate turned, took a step forward and cursed. The entrance was now flashing red. Checking her magic, her eyebrows raised, she said, "But I think we're almost there, it's extremely bright now, so…"

She indicated the far wall, where a series of rotating devices gave the impression of a room that could operate as she started spinning them, checking for patterns again and looking at what I now saw to be old runes or some sort of hieroglyphs along the metal lines between bricks.

The sex stories started up again, this time Goldi talking about how she liked one of her bears whose tongue could work wonders. Hekate squirmed, and Elisa sat there with an amused expression, eyes moving to me once.

In fact, the story was making me want to bury my face in Elisa's pussy right then and there, and if not for the looming danger, I definitely would have.

"Through," Goldi said, opening the final lock. Sure enough, the door slid open. Only, on the other side was nothing but an empty room. "What the hell is this?"

"It's showing that she's here," Hekate said.

"She?" I asked.

Hekate looked at me with a playful smile, nodded, and stepped forward. She lifted the golden feather and started a chant, moving her other hand along the wall.

"If we came all this way for a faulty spell…" Goldi said, voice not even bothering to hide her irritation.

"Trust me, we didn't," Hekate replied, not stopping in her inspection.

"But that's the problem, isn't it?" Goldi replied. "I have no reason to trust you."

"Wrong." Hekate knelt holding the feather up. "You have no past experience leading you to trust me, but every reason to do so."

Gold frowned, apparently not sure how to take this, and folded her arms as she watched.

I glanced around, sure I was hearing sounds in the distance, likely of more gods or Shades coming our way. If we didn't make it out of here, I'd be leaving behind Pucky and the others. We'd barely had a chance to really get to know each other. Me and all of them, really, and Sharon and I had only really just started getting intimate. The idea that it would end there and never with getting a chance to simply go on a date, to spend an evening relaxing without worrying about leveling up or killing gods… it ate at me.

Right there, I swore that if we did make it out of that temple, I'd spend every chance I could getting to know my team, enjoying their company, and not always in a sexual way. Though, knowing them and their appetites, we'd have plenty of that.

The thought caused my eyes to wander to Elisa. She'd knelt, bending over to check for magic in her own way, giving me a nice view of her ass in that blue skirt of hers. A glance back and she smiled, moving her ass back and forth, causing me to blush and find it impossible not to imagine sliding in from behind, hands caressing her back, slapping her ass.

She stood, stepping over to me, and ran a hand to my ass. Leaning in, she whispered, "You can even think of sex in a place like this?"

"With you as company… Anywhere."

The kiss on my cheek was perfect.

"Ladies and gents," Hekate said, completing her spell in a way that caused purple light to form the frame of a door. With another wave of her hand, the door swung inward. "I give you the Golden Goose."

On the other side of that door wasn't exactly what I'd been expecting, but a woman… kind of. She had womanly characteristics, but with gold skin and feathers. Instead of arms, she had wings of gold, and of course a beak where her mouth should have been. Full breasts, shapely hips, and lady parts downstairs.

To make it even weirder, there were two witches with her as she squatted, giving birth to a golden egg. Is that called 'giving birth?' Either way, the egg was coming out of her in a very enticing display.

"What the fuck are you looking at?" the Golden Goose demanded, and the two witches turned in confusion.

"Hekate?" one said, now even more confused. The confusion became even more a moment later, when Hekate stepped in and thrust a glowing white dagger into her throat. No blood came out, only red ichor that Hekate absorbed with a giddy chuckle.

I stepped in to deal with the next witch, sword absorbing her spell and then throwing that magic right back at her the moment I made impact. Black smoke swirled around her, making her rapidly decay until she was dust floating around the ball of ichor that merged with me.

"Oh, fuck," the Golden Goose said, standing there in shock. Her eyes went to each of us, then landed on me. "A bunch of witches and their perverted friend."

"What?" I asked, at first confused about the witch's comment, realizing the illusion was back on. "I wasn't the only one looking, right? Was I?"

It didn't matter, because a swooshing sounded behind us and we spun to see that gods were lining up. Three of them arrived first in golden beams, turning on us for the attack. Seeing Persephone there, I had a feeling this wasn't going to go well.

20

The first wave of gods to attack must have been some sort of enforcers, standing their ground instead of advancing, and throwing up energy shields straight out of a science fiction flick. A god who I guessed to have been Norse based on his long beard and the axe he was wielding started tracing runes in the sky—runes that in turn started creating floating plates of energy that were forming a prison around us. Another appeared behind him, menacing, and carrying a broadsword.

"Heimdall," Elisa shouted at the one with the sword, and then cursed, pushing back along with Hekate.

I didn't know what the hell was going on, but understood that my power was rune based as well, so I figured maybe I could do some damage that way.

Sword drawn, I charged the fast forming prison and started attacking it, so that on my third swing the first of the energy plates broke and caused their spell-caster to stumble back.

It was enough to allow Hekate to get in a blast that sent this Heimdall character staggering back.

"Close them off," the Golden Goose shouted, indicating one of the many screens in this place.

"What?" I shouted, but Goldi was already on it, logging in entering commands, so that as Hekate sent a blast through, the door we'd opened earlier slid shut, cutting us off from the attacking gods.

"Holy balls," Goldi said, still at the screen. "What is this place?"

"What do you mean?" Elisa asked, stepping up next to her.

"I thought it was a prison or something, but—"

"It's so much more," the Golden Goose said. "It's… like a control room."

"No shit," Goldi replied, swiping her hand and then moving back. A full, three-dimensional display shot out in front of her. It showed the pyramid, levels with various blips moving about—most of them gold, and then the room we were in with the red dots that I took to symbolize us. "This is… amazing. It looks like, based on the commands I'm seeing… I can do all sorts of crazy shit."

The Golden Goose took a cautious step toward her. "Be careful, they're not the most forgiving."

Goldi turned to her in shock, seemingly having forgotten she was even there. "Right, yes. And you… You're really here. We need to get you out of this place."

"Please. If you know a way."

Goldi nodded, turning back to the screen. "I'm about to find out. First, to deal with these pests."

The display zoomed in on the area outside our little room, showing the gold of the gods waiting there, as they took on the forms of men and women. With a swipe of her hand, what looked like a laser beam appeared, cutting across the room. She giggled as shrieks sounded from the other side of the door. They might be gods out there but apparently they were being subjected to incredible pain.

She then started rearranging the pyramid as she saw fit, moving traps and changing even the layout of the floors. Our own rumbled as it started to lower, then moved inward and up.

"What're you doing?" I asked.

"Confusing them as much as I can," she replied, and gave me a shrug. "Hell if I know."

Finally she stopped, and then slid open the door as Elisa told us to make a run for it, guiding the Golden Goose as she ran behind.

We were charging out of there and past the maimed bodies of gods. Arms on the floor, one body cleaved in half, and it all smelled of burnt hair and flesh. Halfway back through, going the new route Goldi had cleared for us, we were almost to the center when the lights started appearing again. The gods we'd left behind were upon us.

Heimdall was pulling himself together, healing himself with bursts of light, as he lunged for me with his sword. In his weakened state and me in full health and strength, I was able to parry the strike with my own sword, though his power sent a shock wave through me.

We cleared the first route and started following the Golden Goose until she fell back, screaming, and a new line of gods appeared, unleashing Shades at us. I stepped up, with one hand swinging to take out a shade, with the other calling upon Roar. He burst out and went straight for the gods, while I spun and began hacking away at more Shades. Soon prana was flowing my way again and then a ball of red ichor as Roar tore off one of the gods heads. We were all fighting like trapped animals, but soon Hekate had taken out another of the gods and we at last had a clear path to make it into the next room where we could shut the door, leaving us with only a handful of Shades and one more god to deal with.

We tore through them, my sword ripping the god into three pieces that faded out. More prana and ichor flowed into me as we ran into the next passage, then we found a room.

"Get out of here!" I shouted, Roar and I working to push the door into place.

"I'll get us a portal," Hekate said, moving her hands in a circle to create the portal as I dismissed Roar. We all waited, explosions and shouts sounding like they were coming closer and closer. Only, nothing ever came.

"Hekate!" Elisa shouted, eyes moving to the door.

"It's not working," Hekate cried.

"We need to get off this pyramid, now" the Golden Goose begged. "I'm not going back to them."

With that being said, I pointed to the opening below, past the many ledges leading to open air.

"We jump."

Hekate shook her head. "We need to move faster. I'll make a portal in the air... as long as everyone stays tight, it should work."

"Fuck it," Elisa said with a laugh. "Let them never say I wasn't in for some adventure."

"How far is the center?" Goldi asked.

The Golden Goose cocked her head in thought, then said, "I'm thinking it's right on the other side of these walls. No other reason they haven't come in from that direction yet."

"Let's go for it," I said, and they nodded, all of us up and running, charging through the first door that, indeed, led to the ledge at the center with the massive drop off through the middle of the pyramid.

Elisa was the first up on the ledge, the Golden Goose following right behind with a flap of her wings to get herself into position—and let me say, a nude form crouching like that, ass toward me… not the worst sight in the world. Hekate gave me a nod, but as we made for the ledge, Goldi took a step back.

"Maybe I take my chance with the gods," she said.

"We don't have time for this!" Hekate said, reaching.

"I can fly, but not… like that." Goldi pulled back. "Go to hell. I'm not jumping."

"Your bears are down there," I reminded her, trying to hit that nerve that I knew would do the trick with me. "They'll be waiting for you."

She clenched her jaw, then ran and jumped, straight up to the ledge and over. We all went after her, me letting out an excited yell as the air took me. We passed by explosions and shots from the gods, past balcony's with more of them and their confused faces and even Shades that were starting to charge, to jump after us.

Hekate signaled, and then made her portal directly below Goldi. A split second later, Goldi was gone. We all redirected to the portal, with me being the last. Only, as I passed through it something tugged at my foot and as I adjusted I saw a bright form of purple at my side, coming through with me. I had no idea what or who it was as the light took me, but knew I'd soon find out.

21

Emerging from the portal and into the main room of the mansion, I stumbled at the sight of Persephone on all fours, shaking her head clear. Apparently, she'd been what had latched onto me.

"Oh, shit," Chris said, and I turned to see him and the others charging in. They formed a semi-circle around the room, with me, Elisa, Hekate, and the Golden Goose taking up the defensive and starting to move toward them.

"Anyone but her," Sharon muttered, coming up alongside me and helping me stand. "Wh—what happened?"

"She grabbed hold, but Hekate—"

Hekate was holding her bloodied arm, but shook her head. "We can deal with me after... this."

"You won't be *dealing* with me," Persephone said, finally pushing herself up to stand. She turned to take in her surroundings, then scoffed. "I should've known this would be the place. Ironic, isn't it, that this would be the sight of the final showdown."

"Fuck," Elisa said. "Kill her!"

"It's too late," Persephone said, throwing her arms out to create a shield as attacks came from Red and Hekate simultaneously. "The signal has been sent. Ra and the others will descend on us in no time. And all for what?" She turned to the Golden Goose, scoffing. "Didn't you tell them, you can't make them more powerful?"

"It's not for us," Red said, who was now recovering from being knocked on her ass by Persephone's shield.

"No?" Persephone's eyes landed first on Elisa, then scanned again, slowly narrowing. "Her brothers, but…. There's someone else, isn't there?"

"You'll find out soon enough," Sekhmet said, and she stepped in with Bastet. Gods, was I glad to see them.

At the sight of the two, Persephone stepped back, shield faltering, and she seemed to be preparing to go on the offensive.

"What Persephone is slowly realizing," Sekhmet continued, "is that she's fucked. Isn't that right?"

"The attack is coming," Persephone protested. "I don't have to win, just survive long enough until they get here. Then I'll stand over your corpse and laugh."

"Except that we won't be here," Elisa said.

Sekhmet chuckled. "One thing their kind never understood—a house is just an object. A valuable one in this case, but… it's still just that, not worth protecting if it means any sort of added risk to anyone on our side."

"What are you saying?"

"The portal," Sekhmet said, nodding to Hekate. "Can you get us to a location if I focus on it?" At Hekate's nod, she added, "Do it. All of us."

Sekhmet then lunged for Persephone, Bastet coming around behind her so that when the attack came to fend her off, Bastet was moving in, too. Before she could get involved, though, the Golden Goose spun sweeping a wing out so that one of her feathers flew and brushed against Bastet.

In an instant, the cat was gone, the goddess Bastet stood in her place. Like her sister, she was feline from the neck up, though her gorgeous, nude body was much darker—almost as dark as it could get. Watching her move was paralyzing. At one moment she was amazed to be out of her cat form, the next she was returning to a solid fighting stance, breasts swaying with the movement. Her magic pushed Persephone forward and countered her spell. Sekhmet spun and grabbed her, thrusting her into Hekate's new portal as we all went through.

We emerged on the side of a hill, tall eucalyptus trees surrounding us and a city visible in the distance. Also, I detected a movement of something like a shadow, but in the air.

"This is the spot," Sekhmet said, pinning Persephone down with one hand, her other taking one of her layers of dress from her shoulders and tossing it to her sister.

"Thank you," Bastet said. It was a regal expression, one directed at all of us, though her eyes finally landed on the Golden Goose, and she gave a nod.

"Well, Golden Goose," Elisa said. "Are you ready?"

"Please, call me, Huera," the Golden Goose replied.

Elisa nodded, and Huera stepped forward, ready to go through the portal. Taking my eyes from the now covered form of Bastet, who was openly eyeing me, making my staring very awkward, I first let them roam back over Huera, then quickly remembered myself and stared at the ground. Fuck, with all these beautiful women around, and especially when there was nudity involved, I might as well have gotten a blindfold.

Before anyone had a chance to comment, though, if they had noticed, Persephone roared, struggling to break free. She almost made it, lunging away from Sekhmet, when Sharon was there with a good kick in the face.

"You're not winning this time," Sharon said, and transformed into her large wolf form, leaping to tackle the goddess, both rolling down the hill to slam into a tree. As the rest of us started to react, Sharon shouted, "She's mine!"

And we all backed off, though my hand didn't leave Excalibur. If there was even a chance Sharon would get critically hurt in this fight, I planned on intervening before that happened—her request be damned.

The two circled, Persephone doing her own transformation now. One moment she was a tall, slender woman, the next swirling black smoke took her leaving a demonic being in her place. She still had a womanly feel to her, but was twice as tall, with purple and blue flames coming from her eyes and hands, shadow forming black armor and long claws. They met in a blast of energy and raw power, neither falling back but the rest of us being pushed away, having to throw up shields and defenses to keep from being harmed.

A side of Sharon I'd never seen was coming out,

and it was much more than simply being the large wolf I knew she could be. When her attacks hit, it was with a force of shadow magic, a blast that exploded on impact. Each hit served as a reminder that Persephone and the other so-called gods were indeed nothing more than very powerful fairy tales. That, or Sharon was more godly than we expected, because she was kicking the other woman's ass.

Blood sprayed when Sharon tore out a chunk of Persephone's bicep, but then the weirdest thing happened—the blood flowed back into the woman. Triggered, the goddess's eyes lit up and the fire struck Sharon, so that the wolf fell back, whimpering and rolling.

"Enough," I growled, charging forward.

Red caught me, shaking her head and pointing. Sure enough, Sharon was back up and on Persephone, the flames turning a dark, almost purple shade. The Big Bad Wolf looked like a hell hound, and now the flames actually seemed to be hurting the goddess.

I stepped back, lowering my sword and watching with amazement. Persephone started darting about in jolting teleportation spells, it seemed, but she couldn't shake Sharon off. At last she reached out and summoned a sort of fiery spear, which she managed to use to whack the wolf aside. She held it high and charged, but just before contact Sharon returned to human form and rolled out of the way, then turned back into a wolf as she lunged, catching the demon goddess by the arm and, this time, tearing it completely off.

"Your wolf's a badass," Chris said at my side.

I grinned, then gave him a nod. "All of these ladies are."

"Fucking right," he said, holding out a fist for me to pound while Sharon tore into Persephone, teeth ripping flesh, and blood spraying everywhere. Fuck it, I pounded his fist again with a chuckle. As gruesome as the sight was, I felt relieved to see the so-called goddess bled like the rest of us.

Finally, Persephone went limp and Sharon had her jaws open around the woman's head when Red shouted, "That's enough!"

Sharon turned on her, snarling.

Red took a step toward them, careful not to slip on the hillside. Hand out, she said, "Sharon, you do this, there's no coming back. Remember, you're on the side of right now."

"Come on," Pucky interjected, holding out a hand. "Get back over here, we'll take care of the rest."

Sharon still didn't look convinced, long teeth

exposed and saliva dripping down onto the tattered goddess. After a moment of this, though, her eyes met mine. I nodded, offering a smile.

That's all it took, apparently, to tip the scales. A moment later she was walking toward me with clothes hanging, torn from her transformation, blood along her chin. It was disturbing… and kind of hot.

Meanwhile, Sekhmet and Bastet moved in, working their magic to bind the goddess.

"Hurry," Red said, ushering us on. "We'll keep her in check."

Elisa nodded, motioning me to come along, the Golden Goose in tow, and a moment later we were crossing into the shadow to go back to the Fae world.

As soon as we were through, one of Elisa's brothers was signaling the others. They sprung up from their camp, Arthur, Nivian, and a moment later the fairy queen with them.

Eyes moving to Huera, all stared in awe.

"This is… her?" Elisa's oldest brother asked.

Huera nodded, giving them a bow.

"We can find clothes," Arthur said, looking around as if he expected to spot extras right there.

"Don't be ridiculous," Huera said, and laughed. "I

have no use for such frivolities. Now, who here is in need of my services?"

"All of us," Arthur said.

"And… quicker is better," Elisa noted, glancing back at the portal.

Huera stepped up to Arthur first, holding out her wing. "A fresh feather, given by me. It contains the magic."

"Not the eggs?" I asked.

She turned to frown at me, and laughed. "Oh, gods no. Those contain a different magic altogether."

"I have to pluck a feather?" Arthur asked.

She nodded. "If you were to take one without permission, or try, anyway, your hand would become stuck to me, and anyone who tried to help you, stuck to you. It's a messy and complicated affair, but one we don't have to worry about here. I only have a limited number until they have to grow back,

"What about the snakes and leaves thing, like before?" I asked.

Arthur shook his head as he selected a feather. "This isn't the same—that has to deal with bringing people back from the dead, in a sense. Here, we're spirits without bodies, mostly." As the feather came loose, gold light flowed from it, circling him with tiny specks like dust reflecting in the sun but so much brighter. It then flowed into him, and he was no longer glowing blue and semi-translucent, but complete with a real body, a slight golden glow to his skin.

Nivian embraced him, the two kissing while Huera stepped towards Elisa's brothers next. Two of them went through the same routine before Red appeared in the portal.

"It's time. We have company."

Arthur glanced back at Huera and Queen Mab, the latter waving him off. "Go, fight. Save the world. We'll be right behind you."

Nivian nodded, and we ran to join Red.

"Hurry, brothers," Elisa called back over her shoulder, "I'll be anxiously awaiting your arrival."

We emerged back onto the hillside to find it much darker than before.

"You made it just in time," Sekhmet said, and then pointed up, as if I could've missed the mass of pyramids forming overhead. They're coming from the Fae world, Queen Mab said, and I turned to see her stepping toward us from the portal.

"This is from the spirit realm?" I asked.

"We have a whole underground system of buildings like this," she said, frowning. "Now it explains where they've been hiding, and why the underground has been inaccessible for so long."

"And where all the Shades were going," I said, watching as streams of darkness flowed down toward us, descending with gods and Legends held on high.

I'd said this and turned back to the queen to see her reaction, but froze in confusion. While before she'd looked every bit the fairy queen, as I watched she was growing long, curved horns from her head, her cheekbones becoming more pronounced, lips fuller.

She reached up and touched her mouth, hand then going to the base of one of the horns. "Ah, I see my own glamour has been removed as I was granted access." She held out her arms in the ways she often did, and bowed her head slightly.

"Maleficent?" Elisa asked. "I thought we had her locked up."

"Queen of the fairies, aren't I?" Queen Mab, or apparently Maleficent, said. "Queen Mab tried to invade my dreams once and I couldn't exactly have that, so... yes, I took her ichor, took her essence and use it as glamour when the time's right. Helped me escape, but now I'm here, ready to help."

"Wait, so..." I glanced from her to Red and the others. "Maleficent, good or bad?"

Elisa cocked her head, not really sure how to answer that. Given that the others were looking to her, I took this to mean nobody really knew anymore. Or weren't ready to answer with her watching.

"You see," Maleficent said, stepping toward me, "the answer to your question might have been quite different if you'd asked anytime before we witnessed this." She turned back up to the sky, watching the plumes of Shades, closer now, almost upon us. "That was before I found this. I knew someone was taking a large portion of my fairies, but to turn them into Shades? To spew them out at Earth like they're no better than bullets? Yeah, I mean to have words with those behind the attack. And by words, I mean tear them to shreds."

"I... good."

She smiled, looking around at our little army, and then nodded. "Let's go kick their asses, shall we?"

"But the fairies..."

"Unfortunately, gone." Her eyes showed a sorrow very out of place on her. "The moment they went over, the moment they became Shades, they were lost to me. Gone, forever."

Without another word on the matter, we turned toward the incoming enemy as the rest of our team strode out from the portal, joining us at our sides. And by the rest, I mean *all* of them. Elisa's brothers and all. I quickly applied my previously earned ichor, glad to see I was able to get the skill that cancelled out powers nearby. No luck on the illusion one yet, but it would be up next.

For now, it was fight time.

22

In the face of the onslaught, I called forth Roar. Together we stood our ground with my team, my runes glowing bright and Excalibur charging up with energy. Sharon took up the other side in full wolf mode, while Pucky's horns were glowing where she stood to my left and behind. Red's robe was already flapping about, preparing for the attack.

Elisa charged past, only she didn't have the same look as before. Instead, the white light I'd seen her use previously seemed to have formed into protective armor that gleamed like the moon. In one hand she held a spear of the same material, a shield in the other, with a swan-like helmet on her head.

Her brothers' armor was extending, glowing in

this same way as they charged, and meeting the enemy in a clash of light versus darkness.

I started to charge, too, but caught wind of my name and turned to see Maleficent gesturing to the Arthur who had risen into the sky, a new sword of golden light in his hand. Sekhmet and Bastet were both in animal forms running past me with streaks of magic gleaming in their wake, and then a flurry of fairies came flying out of the portal, moving to intercept the enemy.

"It's going to be a fun fight!" Maleficent said, laughing as she caught up with us, and I continued my charge, Roar pounding along at my side.

The Shades swept over us in waves of darkness, but we were the bulwark that kept them at bay. My team was the staff of Moses that parted the waters, and as I glowed with my rune power—absorbing water for more energy, pulling it from ground and air—prana flowed down to me and I used it to strengthen my connection with Roar, to keep us strong. When I could, I'd duck and quickly assign points, to the extent that soon my strength was at five-hundred percent and my speed at four-hundred. But seeing the host arrayed against us, it was clear where the points really needed to go—stamina. It was all a blur, but I remember at one point getting my stamina to a thousand percent and then watching it flash green, refusing to go higher. Maxed out!

More of the Shades came and we fought, and as I pushed more prana into Roar, a strange thing started happening. I could see from his eyes, sense with his senses. It didn't take away from my own, rather amplifying them to make me more aware of my surroundings. That made me sure it was a smart move, so I started funneling more prana his way, and in a flash he spun, wings out and slicing through the enemy as if they'd taken on a weapon ability of their own. Hot damn, this was going to be fun if I could level up both myself and him, basically surrounded by an endless supply of prana.

Pucky was nearby, shooting her huge-ass rifle at anything she could. I even caught sight of Ali Baba, who I'd lost track of in all the chaos and maneuvering. He had his genie magic going, swirling around enemies, turning them into wind-up toys when he could, shooting out attacks at those powerful enough to resist his simple tricks.

Meanwhile, Elisa and her brothers were tearing through the enemy, making a show of it. You could almost say they were stealing my prana, since at this point it was feeding their armor, making them hulk out. Pretty badass. I spun, avoiding a strike from one and then retaliating with my blade, and watched as a red cloak moved through the crowd, the large wolf that I knew to be Sharon close behind.

Again I swiped at the air, not even bothering to aim this time, and managed to hit one of those fucks. Two came at me at once with strikes that might have done damage if not for my shield flashing up, and then I knelt, coming under a dark shadowy form to shoot out with my group attack. At least ten prana orbs shot my way, and I assigned them to speed.

The momentary distraction wasn't smart though, because I barely had time to register the way the Shades were parting, the form of Heimdall blasting down with his rainbow light and massive sword.

Good thing I had my lion upgrades, because it was through Roar's eyes that I saw it, because of him that I was able to drop and roll to the side to avoid the first blow. My sword was up in time to parry the next strike, and the third met my shield—blasting it to pieces!

Damn, I didn't know if that would need a recharge or if it was gone forever, but either way it wasn't good.

"Mortals," he said, bringing his sword up in a swing that should have been impossible with a blade that size, "will never be able to stand against gods!"

"Good thing you're just a cocky, arrogant, fucking dickhead then," I replied, and thrust out, using my skill to shoot a blade of light. When he dodged in a flash, I considered cancelling out skills to see if that would put us on even footing, but he was twice my size and using a sword he'd likely been training with for hundreds or thousands of years, depending on whether he was an original or not. Instead, I opted for attacking his ego. "You're not a god, you're a pissant, pea-brain jerk who thinks he's better than everyone."

I went on the attack, hoping the words plus my aggression would trigger something in him. It worked. He roared, coming to meet me in a charge, and our swords collided in a burst of colors and energy that sent us both back. Wispy hands gripped me but Roar was there, tearing through them, then looking at me in a way that made me understand. He would hold off the nearby Shades while I took care of Bobby-Big-Balls over there. I nodded, turning to get back into the fight.

Another thing about my moment with Roar. I was reminded that I didn't have to rely only on my senses. Taking that into account with this Heimdall guy's rage, a plan began to form.

This time when we clashed swords and I called him weak, said any of my team could take him, I let him catch me with his sword, barely, making sure I turned so that it was the broadside. The impact sent me flying, landing facing away from him with my sword skittering across the ground.

But that's exactly what I wanted.

Using Roar's senses I knew he was coming at me, and holding out my hand I prepared. When he was lunging, sword coming down for my neck, I summoned my blade, caught it, and turned with a thrust up and kick to his legs.

He went sprawling, sword going up under his sternum so that I could leverage that and throw him over me, sword still in him. Then I was up, summoning it to me, but jumping so that I was taken to it instead. I let the impact do the work, my weight and gravity pushing the blade in deeper, so that I could see his red eyes fade to empty, black sockets as his life force faded. Then he was gone, his ichor entering me.

Without hesitation, I upgraded to get the illusion skill. I had no idea what would come next, and I needed to be ready.

Just then, Huera came charging past with Pucky and Toewi, in pursuit of a group of Shades, while behind me I realized the enemy was clearing enough that I could make out Sekhmet and Bastet where they fought, the others on the far side of them.

We were winning, at least for the moment. Mowgli and the others had joined us and were leading an attack that pushed the Shades away to the East, another group, including Chris's, had moved the enemy on the west back to the bottom of the hill. My group had the immediate north and south handled.

But the darkness surged, a form appearing in the sky. It descended toward us, and all of the surviving enemy backed up, awaiting their ally.

Ra! He'd arrived.

23

R a stopped not far out, close enough to throw a stone at, with my upgraded strength, anyway. He sneered at us, translucent hawk wings out behind him, his helmet glowing like the sun.

"You've returned," he said, turning to assess us all. I wasn't sure who he was addressing, but the statement applied to many of us. "Do you really think you have a chance of standing against me?"

Without waiting to see if anyone else would answer, I shouted out, "I'm the Protector. I will protect."

"You, boy?" He gestured out to the world. "You owe them no loyalty—they'll destroy each other just as they'd destroy all of us! I've lived among them, I know."

"It's never too late to make a change." I stepped forward, hating how I sounded like a motivational poster. "In this case, the change starts with you backing off… or dying."

He scoffed. "You're in no position to threaten me. My forces surround the world."

"And yet, I'll bet they'll fall back the moment I've taken your head."

"You…?" He scoffed. "You're like a little baby compared to me, you with that sword—you're as likely to cut off your own scrotum as scratch me. You, a Protector? Join me, I'll train you. I'll show you what being a Protector really means."

"I know what it means well enough."

"Clearly, you don't." He moved closer, eyes boring into me. "I am a god, yes, but also a Legend, if you must call it so. Your kind were meant to protect us all, to see that humanity can't touch us."

"I'm here to protect your kind, yes." I stepped forward, again, not wanting to seem like I was the backing down type. "In this case, that means protecting both fairy tales and humanity in one… against you."

"Well then…" He held out his hands, a sudden rush of gods appearing at his side. An army like that of heaven about to descend on us. Shit, it was intimidating. "Prepare to die, Protector."

He brought his hands forward and the gods streamed down on us. To her credit, Maleficent was the first one to charge this time, her fairies streaming up with her in a blinding effect that let her attack hit the mark on two gods right off the bat. Sekhmet and Bastet were right behind her, so I got the idea that the gods were taking the brunt of the attack from us "non-gods."

But I wasn't about to stand for that—I was going to take my share of the blows, dammit. Running up to the first god to land, I met him in combat while Elisa took out one who was coming in at me from above.

"Thanks!" I shouted, and the blast that I sent through this god was enough to stun him until I'd slashed his throat open with my blazing blue blade.

Attacks came at me that I absorbed, using the energy for a group attack, then running to help defend Huera as she healed two of Elisa's brothers. My whole team was in the process of moving together, forming a wedge, while the gods kept the enemy from getting behind us. Spells were flying, Chris and the others making their way back to us and half-way up the hill, Mowgli and the other Myths doing their best to join forces as well. The gods were working to keep us separated, Legends were mostly being used as cannon fodder so that flying monkeys, trolls, and various others, like Rumpelstiltskin, were falling dead in droves. A few Myths fell, too, but so far none of my own team, and none that I knew by name.

A roar sounded, then two more, and I glanced back to see three large bears, one with Goldi locks on his shoulder. She held a bazooka, which she fired into the sky. The explosion hit the closest pyramid, sending a large section of it down to crush the enemy beneath it. Goldi and her crew came charging, others with rifles and more following. From what I could tell, this new group wasn't even fairy tale.

Jets streaked overhead in the distance, laying down the attack on the buildings in the sky, but one vanished.

"The normies are back at it, at least," Red said, momentarily appearing at my side. "They're seeing our fight and rallying to the cause."

"About time," I grumbled.

Maybe they could at least serve as a distraction, but as few normie lives lost during the process, the better. I'd never understood the idea of valuing civilian lives more than those of the military, but now that I was there in the midst of a battle, it started to make sense. We were there to give our lives, if that's what it took. Every one of us was there to sacrifice so that others didn't have to, which meant that every life lost 'back home' was another loss to our cause, another reason our sacrifice, if it came to that, would mean that much less. Our lives weren't less valuable, but if I were to die there on the battlefield, so be it. As long as my death resulted in less chance of success for the enemy, and in less death back home.

Not that I could compare myself to those men and women in the military, I thought with a laugh. They'd been doing this for years, training and fighting for our lives and freedom, and here I was like a baby in the grand scheme of it all.

Then again, I was going for the end game. Whatever it took to grow, to make myself the ultimate warrior… I'd do it.

Maybe when this was all over, I'd find a way of changing how the system worked. I could partner with the police, the Marines, all of them, and combine their discipline and firepower with my use of the supernatural. A conversation for another time, of course, because at the moment I was staring down a goddess who'd decided I was her next target. Then another. Then a third. All stared at me, slowly stepping closer, weapons drawn.

I recognized them, maybe from a show I'd been watching recently and then read about online? I wasn't sure, but seeing them there with their gowns of stars and planet patterns, their curved blades, and the way their eyes seemed dark and full of the stars.

Confirming my guess, a voice said, "That's the Evening Star on the right." A moment later, Maleficent was there at my side, materializing next to me with a flash of purple and fairies darting about her. "I'll take her."

That left the Morning Star and the Midnight Star. Cool, I could try for two ancient goddesses. Why not?

"Good to see you," I said to the queen of fairies, pushing energy into my sword and preparing for the charge.

She nodded, then pointed to my left. Crows were coming together in that spot, a moment later forming into Toewi.

"The one on the left?" Toewi asked with a wink.

Both of my new friends flew forward in bursts of darkness and color, but I had to rely on my feet to charge. Roar joined me, and I leaped up onto his back so that when I met the Morning Star in a clash of swords, it was leaping from Roar's back and striking as I fell. She parried the blow with a flash of light that left me seeing spots, but my lion attacked her from the other side and gave me time to recover.

Remembering that I had my illusion skill now, I

pushed it out so that it seemed there was three more of me crouching there. She struck, blade gleaming as it cut through the watery mist of my illusion, leaving her open for my strike. My blade slid along her arm, cutting a thin line along her cheek.

She was fast, but silver blood dripped down to her jaw, telling me she wasn't invincible.

"Who the fuck do you think you are?" she said, touching the blood, eyeing it, and then flicking it aside. Interestingly, it never touched the ground, instead floating off and becoming one with the air.

"Just Jack," I said with a grin, and attacked again.

This time her confidence was down, a fact made even more true by her buddy yelping in pain as Maleficent broke the goddess's arm. When I came in for a strike, she flinched and I faked with the sword to, instead, catch her with sweep of the legs that sent her to the ground. She flew out of the way of my sword as I brought it down, as if space had moved her on its own, but Roar was on it, darting left and coming back in to maul her as Toewi cast a spell that hit her goddess and mine with black roots from the ground, holding them in place.

Mine screamed as Roar did his thing, and then I came in for the final swing.

Head removed, she didn't seem so badass anymore. Toewi had pulled two short, curved daggers from her belt and quickly ended hers as well. Morning Star and Midnight Star were both gone, their ichor flowing into us—one each.

"Sorry, was I supposed to give you that?" Toewi asked.

I laughed, dodging out of the way as the Evening Star's arm went flying by. "No, I don't know why my team always does. They need it too, I should think."

She nodded. "Next time, just let me know."

We both turned to help Hekate, but she was standing with both hands in the goddess's chest, silver blood washing over her, taking on her form. I shrugged, figuring it was done, but Toewi cursed and charged in.

I was confused, but when Toewi grabbed Hekate and there was no reaction, I realized that silver blood must've had some power of its own. Toewi had both hands on Hekate, then, but seemed to be losing her focus as well, eyes going distant.

Without a clue of what to do here, I saw Arthur land nearby with his blade of light cutting a god in half, then spinning to cut through two more.

"Arthur!" I shouted, and a moment later he was at my side, Nivian following closely.

"This isn't good," he said, but turned to me. "Together, okay?"

"I…" Images of that silver blood taking over me,

moving into me and filling every orifice tore through my mind. But what could I do? I nodded, reaching out with him.

"Focus on your Tempest abilities," he said. "And on me."

We laid hands on them and I felt like the damn Brer Rabbit with the tar, even feeling the silver enter me. It was too strong, even with my focus on Arthur and our connection to the elements. My energy was being sucked out, any connection with who I was.

Except, I still had unused ichor, and Roar was nearby. Focusing on that, I channeled myself into him, helping to break the bond the silver had on us. There it was like I was sitting on Roar's back, and Arthur was suddenly with me, and we were staring at the goddess with darkness and discs floating all around, as if the three of us were in space. She turned her attention to us, and I was about to attack but for a hand held up from Arthur.

"This one's not physical, friend," he said.

Understanding, I focused more of my energy into the link and our powers, and as she started to scream, to break apart, the link broke in a flash of silver. Thrust out of this other plane, we all fell to the ground, all but Maleficent and the goddess.

The difference though, was that now Maleficent was herself again. She chanted, runes appearing around her forearms, silver receding. A moment later, the goddess exploded into nothing, leaving only the ichor behind.

She waved it toward me, collapsing to one knee. But I waved it back to her, pushing it in as I helped her to stand. "You need it more."

"You…" She shook her head, then smiled. "I might have underestimated you."

Toewi was looking at me with awe, too. "We'd be goners if not for you."

"And Arthur, and Roar," I said.

"You named your lion, your spirit animal… Roar?" Toewi laughed, then threw her arms around me. "You're weird, but… thank you."

All around us the fighting continued, and we could see the agents and military fighting the enemy in the distance, Chris and his witches having finally joined up with us.

But my attention was directed toward an ominous presence overhead, where a hawk flew, screeching out in a way that caused all of the gods to look up in reference to their leader, to Ra.

"I got this," I said with the rush of our recent victory running through me, and leaped onto Roar's back. His wings spread wide and he ran, pounding and then took off into the sky. Excalibur at the ready, I stared at the god above, totally wondering what the hell I was getting myself into.

We circled each other, him sending wave after wave of attack my way in the form of solar blasts. The only reason I was able to survive was thanks to Roar and the high amount of water I could call on up here. It was like riding waves, the two of us diving around Ra, always on the move, trying to get in hits. I'd shoot with my sword, sending gleaming blades of light his way, then come in for a strike, but couldn't land a damn thing.

Each of his attacks left the air below scorched, and with each miss of mine I started to lose confidence.

"What do we do here, Roar?" I asked.

He roared.

And actually, that was the answer I needed. We didn't need to charge up here and beat him as if I were his equal. We had a team, sure, but they were pretty damn occupied below. What I needed was to get him down to my level, and the best way I could figure making that happen at the moment was to roar as loud as I fucking could.

"Come and get me, you son of a bitch!" I shouted, flying past him and then guiding Roar toward the nearest pyramid, the one that had been hit earlier and had a good chunk of it missing. Chancing a glance back to see if he took the bait, I saw him following, and grinned.

Maybe this would result in my death, but hey, I hadn't died so far. As far as I knew and hoped, it simply wasn't my fate to die. More strikes came my way, but we had a destination now and made it, me jumping from Roar's back and dismissing him, turning with sword raised.

There was only one way this could work, so as soon as Ra was within range, I activated the skill that would cancel out both of our powers. It was like I was squeezed dry, suddenly empty. While before I could sort of sense everything going on around me, feel my powers as one can smell and hear and see… now it was simply me. Nothing else.

Judging by the confused look in Ra's eyes as he fell to the platform in front of me, the way his hawk wings vanished and the glow around his hands faded, it had worked.

With a rush, no powers here, only me versus him—man to man—I collided with Ra as he once was, as he was before he became this god. The man Arthur had known once as Pinocchio, with just hints of Torrind, the agent, whose body he'd taken over before that, but all of Ra fading. He was screaming, clawing, biting. Doing anything he could to try and fight me off, but even without using powers, I'd grown strong and learned a thing or two.

His strikes were easily blocked, my punches landing well. I kicked him back toward the edge of the platform, then came in for another kick that sent blood flying into the open sky. When he turned back to me, however, he had a wild, excited look.

"You thought it would be so easy?" He rotated, throwing himself over.

For a second I stared in confusion. But of course it wasn't going to be that easy, and I realized this when I ran to the side and looked over, watching as other gods flew into him, giving themselves to him so that a moment later wings sprouted out—otherworldly, unholy wings that seemed to be made of skin and exposed flesh. He floated up toward me, long horns growing from his forehead, shoulders, back, and even a tail.

While he might not have been truly evil before, this creature he was devolving into clearly was.

"I have to ask myself," he said in a thick, burning voice, "why bother with you when killing everyone on your team first would bring me so much more joy?"

He spun back toward the ground, where Huera was flying about in the fight, to where I could see Sharon the wolf engaged in battle against a

Cerberus. And then he dove, bursts of lightning crackling as he prepared the attack.

"Roar!" I shouted, and ran and jumped, hoping my lion would be there. Air flew past, my panic rising as I descended, and then suddenly Roar was there, beneath me, catching me and continuing the dive. My sword flew to my hands, and I slashed in the air, sending blasts of light at the creature that had been Ra.

His back arched and he howled in pain, turning as we plowed into him, sword slicing, tearing. But for every strike, his body would grow back. Every time a limb went missing, another of his gods would join him, become absorbed into his body and a mutated lump would appear.

"You winning here is not how this day will go," Ra shouted, coming back with a barrage of attacks that sent me spinning, head splitting in pain.

"If I can just kill you, I'll be happy." I charged back in with Roar, him clawing and biting as I leaped, sword up. With all my might, I thrust Excalibur into Ra as I fell.

The momentum and gravity brought me down, sword continuing to tear through Ra until he was cleaved in two, light bursting forth and taking me. Only, I wasn't falling anymore, and as my eyes began to see in the brightness, a form lunged at me.

A short, wooden boy! Hit fist slammed into my gut, the light fading to no more than a bright light in the mists, and there was Pinocchio, staring up at me with hatred. Slowly, his eyes lowered to take in the fact that he was a nude, wooden puppet, and he shouted, "What have you done to me?"

"Brought you to justice," I replied, and then shoved him back, Excalibur pointed. "It ends here."

"You piece of shit. I'm a god now, not some wooden toy. I'll tear you to shred, fucking splinter you to death!"

He came at me again, this time pulling in the mists around as runes on his wooden body glowed. The mists swirled, assaulting me like shards of glass —shards that never hit their target, thanks to my raised shield that I formed form my arm.

While he clearly still had power, it wouldn't be enough. I'd trained in the mists enough to know my way around. To know that they could be my ally.

I spun, taking the mists and swirling them around myself so that I returned the attack. Only instead of the assault like glass, I took it to the next step, pushing the mists together so that the water hardened, even formed a sort of massive axe that swung for the wooden boy. He stumbled back and held up his hands, runes glowing, and the two of us were locked like that, mentally pushing, my will against his.

It took everything I had, focusing on all of my training with Arthur, on the energy I'd received through powering up and grinding. But most of all, what got me through that moment was thinking about my team, about Pucky, Red, Elisa, Sharon, and now the others joining us.

Was love the secret ingredient? Fuck if I know, but it sure as hell kept me sane as Pinocchio attempted to win over my mind with mental attacks.

No matter what, I had to return to my team. To be there for them, to ensure they were all right. And yes, the thought crossed my mind—to make sweet love to them all again. No way was I going to lose here and die knowing they'd be eagerly awaiting their hero.

Taking a gamble, I thrust out with my power-cancelling skill. The effect was immediate, mists exploding out, or so I thought. As the light started to return, I saw that my attack had hit its mark before being cancelled by the lack of powers.

Then the light was surrounding us, taking over so there was nothing but the light, and I was falling.

Wind tossing me about, light going in and out, all I knew was that falling sensation. Then I processed that Roar was there, catching me on his back. I could see again, and noticed Huera flying alongside us, casting her healing spell.

"Where…?" I asked, summoning back my sword so that it flew to my hand from where it had been tumbling down.

She gestured to a cloud of ash in the sky, being blown away by the wind. "You mean Ra? Gone, thanks to you."

I watched as the ash circled, forming a small tornado before blowing away. So went Ra, the great god, the man, the agent… the boy of wood. Finally, gone.

24

Pyramids were falling all around us, exploding, crashing—only, not making impact but vanishing as they hit the ground. Or that's what I thought at first as I descended, caressing Roar's mane to show him how much I appreciated his help.

One of the larger pyramids was hitting nearby, but I watched as it made impact to see that there was an opening between worlds, another land being torn apart as the pyramid hit and exploded. Was it the Fae world, the place underneath, or some other place I hadn't learned about yet?

I was curious, but based on the adventures I'd been on so far, I had a feeling this would be revealed in time as well. When we landed next to the others, I took a moment to look around at them, taking stock.

"Where's Pucky?" I asked.

Elisa was being helped up by one of her brothers, and Red landing nearby. Sharon shook her head, and my heart froze.

"Behind you," Pucky's voice came, and I turned to see her holding her side, one of her horns broken off, blood on her forehead, but otherwise unharmed. "Don't look so distraught, it'll grow back. Eventually."

"Maybe he's making that face because, with just one of them, it kinda looks like a cock growing out of your head." Red laughed, and then stumbled.

Pucky half-teleported to her side, catching her. "You're hurt. And a bitch."

Red chuckled, softer than her previous laugh, and moved her cloak aside to reveal a nasty gash on her side. It looked bad, but she was standing strong. "We did well, didn't we?"

"We won," I said, going to her side for support.

"And… what next?"

"Next we get you to a doctor," I replied, trying to figure out how best to deal with the wound in the meantime. Apply pressure? I'd heard that in movies, but it wasn't like I was trained in first aid or anything like that. We would have to add that to the training when we got back.

"No need," a soft voice said, and we turned to see

Huera, golden breasts seeming to glow in the waning sun. "I can see to it."

"At what cost?" I asked.

"No cost," Huera replied, stepping up in front of Red. "I can give each of you a healing ability, though it's not quite god status. That... I've used up, until more feathers grow." She indicated her wings, where several bare patches showed at the bottom of each. "But what I'm talking about is something different, something much easier. Bring me into the team."

Pucky and Elisa exchanged a curious look, while Red pursed her lips and Sharon actually glared.

"To be clear," Red asked, "you'd want to be part of *this* team? I mean, the Protector's team?"

Huera nodded. "And when it's time, you can all become gods—as our definition of that goes, anyway. You'll become much harder to kill, and receive other benefits. But for now, yes... If we're intimate, you get a slower-acting healing affect, one that would work quick enough to help Red with that whole situation."

The idea of fucking a golden woman with wings and beak was an odd one, but I wasn't opposed to it.

"She's proven herself," Pucky said with a nod to Sharon. "And honestly, you won't lose any affection from Jack. He's shown us that over and over. Trust me."

Sharon looked hesitant.

"We won't do it unless everyone's on board," Elisa added.

With that, Sharon's expression melted and she said, "Fine."

"Yeah?" Huera said, eyes wide.

"I'm game," Red said. "What, I gotta eat some pussy to get healing power? No complaints there."

"That's putting it crudely," Huera said with a frown. "And not exactly how it works."

"Don't mind her," I said with a laugh. "Red's like that sometimes."

Red shrugged, letting out a moan as she gripped her side.

"Maybe we… don't waste any time?" Pucky advised.

As others were starting to check on each other, Huera moved in to do what she could.

"You all do realize we probably have other healers here, too?" Arthur said, but grinned wide. "Not saying this was a bad choice, just wanted to make sure you knew it wasn't the only choice."

"We knew," Red said with a chuckle, hand moving along Huera's hip, closer and closer to the golden landing strip above her pussy. "Or I did, anyway, but thought this way we get to have some fun while we're at it."

Huera looked surprised. "You knew?" She cocked her head, clearly debating whether to be mad or not, but then started laughing—only to be interrupted by a shudder as Red's finger entered her.

"Maybe this should continue at the mansion," I said, noting several other Myths starting to look our way.

"It could," Red replied, wrapping her cloak around herself and Huera. "Or you all could just pretend to not know what's going on under here."

I laughed, looking away. As much as I pretended, though, the pressure in my pants showed I couldn't stop thinking about it. The way Huera was looking at me, too, as she bit her lip and attempted to conceal a moan, made me excited to get in on that situation.

"Everyone's eager to get out of here," Arthur said, not even pretending he hadn't noticed all of this. "Let's all take an hour or two, then meet at Elisa's courtyard, where we can touch base and discuss next steps."

"Next...?" I asked.

He nodded. "Humanity is going to have a tough time with us fairy tales after seeing all of this."

"Can't we just, I don't know—glamour them... flash something in their eyes that makes them forget?"

Arthur frowned, looked around at the others. "It's something we can do, but… on this scale?"

Everyone looked as confused as him.

"Um," Pucky held up a hand, "we'll try, but it might take time. Some of it might stick… we can't be sure."

"Or it might be a bunch of bullshit," Sharon interjected. "The world will finally know us for what we are, which might not be the worst thing in the world."

"How so?" I asked.

"Well, I for one would love to not have to hide who I am. To be able to wear it proudly."

"Me too," Pucky added as she wiped some blood from her forehead. "Imagine a world where this—this… horn, is accepted?"

"We'll have a long way to go before it gets to that," Arthur argued. "But there's no better time than now to start down that path."

Mowgli was heading over to meet us, but Elisa waved for him and said, "I'll hold him off, tell him the plan about meeting at the mansion. Then, let's get to it. I'm… worked up." She winked my way before heading off to intercept the incoming Myths.

"I suppose you'll want my help getting back there?" Hekate asked Toewi, then Huera.

Toewi turned to me and to the other ladies, and

cocked her head. "You know, what you all have… I've always dreamed of it."

Huera nodded, eyeing me contemplatively. "Actually, she has a good point."

"I'm sorry, what point is that?" Elisa asked.

"I was thinking I can help you all out," Toewi said. "If you're taking on new applicants for the team and all."

"New applicants…" Pucky considered them, a hint of a smile on her lips. "You do understand what you're asking to be part of, right?"

The ladies nodded, both eyeing me with added interest.

"New applicants?" Sharon looked worried. "How many new members are we accepting, exactly?"

Pucky was the only one still giving us her attention, though she looked a bit woozy. She smiled my way, laughed, and said, "Hey, more the merrier."

Elisa scrunched her nose, looked at the ladies, and then shrugged. "We can… consider it."

"How many more?" Maleficent asked, glancing at me and then to the ladies. "You know… hypothetically speaking."

"Seriously?" Sharon asked.

"It's better for all of us," Pucky said.

I laughed. "Pucky, I'm starting to wonder who's the most excited about all of this."

"Hey, you don't have to fuck them all if you don't want." Pucky gave me a 'yeah, right' look. "Let me do my thing, we see what happens, and maybe you get curious one night. It'll be fun."

I chuckled, but turned to Sharon. "I wouldn't do anything any one of my team didn't feel comfortable with."

Sharon glared at me as if not sure what to believe, but then turned back to Maleficent and the others. "A trial, okay? This first… time… will be to see how it works out. Nothing more."

"Yet," Pucky added.

"Sure." Sharon allowed a hint of a smile, and for the first time I realized that maybe this didn't totally turn her off, she was just worried what it would mean for us. Well, then, I'd have to make sure she didn't feel the slightest lack of attention when the moment came.

With that, we stepped through the portal back to our mansion, apparently to get the biggest fuck on I'd ever been part of.

25

Back at the mansion, we were caught between a celebration and debriefing of everything that had happened. It seemed that, considering our contribution to defeating the main enemy leading the attack, the agents of the normies were going to lay off of us, even change their stance and start working with Myths instead of Legends. They agreed to work together with Myths to set up rehabilitation centers for Legends and gods alike, and truly attempt to form a livable situation with the fairy tales among them—secretively, of course. It turned out they had their own sort of amplifier that worked to ensure most of the world forgot about what had happened, instead thinking it had been massive natural disasters that had caused havoc.

I spent my first few hours back in a juggle of wanting to get some rest, to making sure the new ladies felt welcome. No, not in *that* way yet, but by getting to know them, even playing a game of Uno with the team. Sharon kept rolling her eyes at it, but when she won she wanted to play again.

At one point, I found Chris dragging me off to stare out over the city with him, and found myself staring at him instead in confusion.

"We have a mansion full of friends, ladies, food… drink!" I laughed. "What're we doing out here?"

"I miss you man." He leaned forward. "Plus," pulling out his pants to show me his dick, which was very swollen and kinda lopsided, "I need you to tell me if this is wrong."

"Fuck yes, that's wrong. Don't ever show me your dick again."

"No, I mean…" He looked at me with such fright, I couldn't help but feel sorry for him.

"Relax, relax, I think it's just swollen. Over-use, right?" I glanced down to confirm, then quickly looked away. "Just, put that nastiness away, man."

He chuckled. "If only it was always that big limp, huh?"

"You're ladies might be complaining. I mean, who wants a soda can for a cock? They want a healthy balance of length and girth. At least I think so."

He nodded. "Fuck."

"What?"

Glancing back at the mansion, he sighed. "Hekate said two new friends wanted to join in today. Some real nasty, freaky witches. But with this… Fuck it, I'm doing it anyway."

"Chris…"

"Joking, joking. Maybe."

I shook my head, laughing, and looked back over the city. "Damn, I wonder how hard I'll have to stare at all this to get that vision of your dick out of my head?"

"Why you thinking about it?" He grinned. "Sorry."

"Man…" I looked down at my thick arms. "I can't believe how far we've come in such a short amount of time. It's insane, right?"

"Fuck yes. I still remember reading Harry Potter and thinking how much I wanted to hit up the Florida park to feel the experience—but now I know that he had it lame compared to this."

"Apples and oranges," I said with a laugh. "And… that was fiction."

"Sure." He winked at me.

Not sure what that meant, I asked, "So you going back to the witches mansion? I mean, what's the plan there?"

"I think so. They're giving it to us, actually, with Hekate as head witch. And, I mean, that only makes sense anyway. It was all political, but she was definitely the most badass."

"And you're learning?"

He nodded. "Watch this." Holding out a hand, he made a little fire appear, then waved his other hand and made it take the shape of a nude woman, then again and he gave it my face. Cracking up as I shoved him, he said, "Hey, not bad man. Your head on a body like that."

"I'd look good no matter what," I admitted, playfully but actually… yeah, the confidence was definitely there now. After the fighting, the leveling up, the fucking? I couldn't imagine how I'd ever lacked confidence in the first place. That guy who'd been doing press at the con was a totally different person.

"Well, I hope we get to hang out often," Chris said, nodding and giving me a big-brother look.

"No doubt," I said. "As long as the violence and all that stays calm, I imagine we won't have much else to do but enjoy ourselves."

"You wish," Pucky said, coming out through the double glass doors. "You're going to be training your ass off, preparing for whatever comes next. And trust me, there's always something next."

I gave Chris a 'there you go' look.

"Come on," Pucky said, pulling me by the hand, giggling.

"What's gotten into you?" I asked.

"Just, hurry."

Chris grinned and followed as Pucky dragged me back through the mansion, downstairs and into the courtyard. There in the waning sunlight all of the fairy tales were gathered, along with some Legends, it looked like, who must've switched sides. If not, I had no idea what they were doing there.

But weirdest still was the fact that I noticed two people I had never thought to see in a place like this, and hadn't actually been sure I'd ever see again at all. My mom and dad.

"What...?" I staggered toward them, then broke out into a run until we were embracing, laughing, and turning to see everyone watching. "What's going on here?"

"Ask her," my dad said, and indicated Pucky. "All of them, I guess."

Indeed, next to Pucky, Red, Sharon, and Elisa had stepped forward. They were in a sort of semi-circle in front of me, the new team members—if they were going to indeed be part of the team, lined up behind them. Even Sekhmet and Bastet were there in the line, as apparently they'd decided they were part of the team. And Maleficent, the Queen of Crows, and

Huera. It was quite the display of beauty, and kind of awkward, since Huera was still apparently refusing to wear clothes.

"Pucky?" I asked.

"We won," Pucky said. "But that's not the only reason to celebrate, we figured. As you know—"

"We love you," Red blurted out, then blushed the color of her hood.

"It's true," Elisa said, nodding.

Sharon cleared her throat. "I never… I never thought it would be possible, especially only knowing each other after such a short time, but when you know, you know."

"There's a spiritual or magical way of telling more than any other way," Pucky said, but then waved off her own comment. "The point is, we do. And…"

She paused, looking at the other ladies.

"We have a question for you," Elisa said, and then nodded. As one, they went to one knee each, then Pucky held out a ring, each of them putting their hands on her arm.

As one, they said, "Jack, will you marry us?"

I nearly choked on my surprise. Maybe I should've seen it coming, but in the normie world, it didn't happen this way. My father was smiling wider than I'd ever seen him smile.

"You knew about this?" I asked.

He winked. "Son, we live in an age where a woman proposing to a man isn't what it once was. Being wanted isn't a bad thing, and being wanted by four stunning women? I'd say you have to be an idiot to turn this down."

My mom hit him.

"Not that I'd ever want more than one," he added quickly. "Hell, how you'll manage is beyond me."

She hit him again, but laughed. "I'm not arguing, but your father likes it when I hit him, so I go along."

"Ah, too much information."

"Jack…" Elisa said, voice low, eyebrows raised. "We're kind of waiting for an answer."

"Oh, damn," I chuckled. "I mean, of course."

Sharon looked up at me, eyes wide. "Wait, that was a yes, right?"

Pucky, even Red and Elisa were there, waiting for an answer. The others would maybe join in too, in time. I had no idea—it was all too confusing. But one thing wasn't confusing in the slightest, and that was my answer.

"Of course, yes." I said. "YES!"

I went to them, helping them up and we were all kissing, then the others were stepping forward, congratulating us, kissing me as well. The whole scene made me feel like I was flying again, so much joy bursting forth that Roar jumped out, soaring around the sky above and roaring, nearly giving my mom a heart attack. My parents were doing fairly well, considering all of this was so new to them, and I looked forward to sitting down with them over a bottle of wine to tell them everything. Well, of course not everything, but as much about this world as I could to help explain.

Fairies appeared around Maleficent, flittering about us with their glowing purples and greens, and a flock of crows flew overhead as the Queen of Crows laughed, throwing her arms around Red.

A lot of these women seemed the most unlikely of friends. The idea of the goth mistress herself, Red, being my lover—or in a shared marriage—with Elisa and Pucky didn't fit, but here it was, happening. Her and Sharon, though? Yeah, that actually seemed like a match. Throw in the queens of fairies and crows, a half goose or whatever Huera was, and the cat and lioness goddesses, and I had one interesting future in terms of relationships. A future I wouldn't change for anything.

EPILOGUE

We didn't waste any time with the wedding—why would we? It was all done per the old ways, with Mowgli making it official and doves released into the sky and all that. No Church or State, since they would've ruled a marriage of this size illegal and the whole idea of the fairy tales existing to begin with was a murky one.

It went by in a blur, me in fancy robes of a Protector that reminded me of a combination between what Prince Aladdin and Prince Charming would've worn at the height of their fame. Flowing robes of royal blue with gold lining, and all that brouhaha that I couldn't give two shits about. What mattered to me was the ladies, and boy did they bring it.

They redid the gardens of Elisa's mansion—I guess our mansion, now—and had a whole crowd of fairy tales gathered. My parents were there in the front row and Chris nearby with his witches, the other members of my team acting as brides maids. Music started and I couldn't tell where from, until I noticed some of it was coming from fairies, but also from several fauns I could just make out sitting amongst the trees.

First down the aisle was Pucky. A diamond studded tiara had been placed just perfectly to cover her recent horn injury, and it complimented the green and blue of her many layered dress. It moved like the wind, with tiny fairies adding an effect like the stars. Nearby, Maleficent gave her a nod, and I figured the two had worked together on the garment.

Next came Elisa in sky blue with white swan motif jewelry and tiara. What struck me the most about her, though, was the way the veil and dress shimmered, reminiscent of the way a cool breeze blows across an otherwise calm lake.

Sharon emerged in a stunning gown of gold and black. Very not what one would expect in a wedding, but for her I thought it was the perfect display of her new life, a mixture of the shadows with light I was glad to see she had already healed from her wounds, completely, as not a scratch showed on her exposed arms or shoulders. Her eyes met mine and the joy that showed there made my knees buckle, so that I had to focus on my breathing. I was actually going to be with these women for the rest of my life! Tingling warmth spread through me, my smile wide.

Finally, Red entered, totally surprising me. No red or even black today, but a very traditional white wedding dress. The only sign of her moniker was the red lipstick, standing out strong against the white. Her breasts—already large—were pressed up for full cleavage effect, but in a classy way that reminded me of what a medieval wedding dress might have looked like. As she drew closer, I realized that was exactly what this was, only pristine. Arthur was looking at it with a special kind of pride, and I had to wonder if he knew something of its origin.

The women were soon at the front of the room with us, their maids of honor beaming, streams of gold, green, and other colors of magical light flowing up as they were unable to control their emotions.

My own emotions flooded, eyes blurry, and all I could do was focus on not letting tears of joy come at the sight of my future. Then Mowgli was speaking the words, someone shouted with excitement, and all of them were kissing me, lifting me in the air, and it was over!

Well, not exactly over, because then came the dancing, the feast, the cake and champagne. Chris lit up the dance floor with his witches, me and my wives holding our own but too focused on trying to ensure everyone else was having a good time and on keeping our emotions in check. Plus, I kept glancing over at my parents, looking forward to the chance to get to talk with them more privately.

The moment came as the reception was coming to an end, and as some of the guests were funneling out, my father found me, guiding me to a side room where my mother waited.

"We're truly proud of you, son," my father said, and he laughed. "Though, truthfully I have no idea how you managed this whole scenario."

"You want to join him, find yourself a little troupe of ladies?" my mom asked, more like giving up than anything. "I'm sure I could do well for myself, too."

He pulled her close, noses almost touching, and said, "Never. All I want is right here, standing in front of me. All I could ever want."

"I love you," she said, and he said it back as they kissed.

A bit too much kissing, honestly, but I let them have it.

When they were done, we embraced, and I told them I'd come visit home soon. After some well-deserved rest. When they were gone, I found Elisa with her brothers, Arthur, and Nivian in the back gardens, where they'd created a portal to the Fae world.

"Perfect timing," Arthur said, gesturing me to come over. "We've already said our farewells to everyone else."

"You're leaving?" I asked.

"We're able to move back and forth at will," Arthur explained, an arm around Nivian. "Whenever you want to visit, to see the civilized part of the Fae world, please, feel free."

I shook his hand and thanked him for everything, then the same for Nivian.

"All set?" Elisa asked, approaching with her brothers. Apparently, they had lives and families in the Fae world that they would be getting back to, but the same applied where they could come and go at will.

"I'm going to miss everyone," I admitted. "What's the world going to be like, now that all of this craziness is over?"

"As it's meant to be," Nivian said, and she gave me a nod before leading Arthur off.

"Take care of our sister," the oldest of Elisa's brothers said, and they each wished us the best before following Arthur back through the portal.

The last of the visitors gone, Elisa winked and said, "Come, follow me."

"I think… I need a nap."

She laughed. "Your business isn't done yet."

Not liking the sound of that, I followed her down the steps and toward the rear drawing room, one of the larger rooms she often used as a studio.

Elisa grinned, wide. "While we're your wives, we couldn't just leave out the rest of them, could we?"

She pulled the curtain aside, and where I'd expected maybe a present or something, instead I found several beds pushed together, and lying on the beds were all of the ladies now on the team. *Completely nude.* There was of course the core team of Pucky, Red, and Sharon—with Elisa moving over to join them. But then, starting to sit and touch themselves and each other while watching me, the row behind my core team was made up of Sekhmet kissing Toewi, Bastet caressing Maleficent, while the latter had her hand between Huera's thighs.

It was like they'd formed an offensive line of love making, ready to conquer me. And I had no doubt they were going to win… in a good way that would allow me to win as well… again and again and again.

"I don't suppose you know anything about a fairy tale wedding?" Maleficent asked as the women moved over to undress me.

I gulped. "Only the happily ever after part."

"Oh, we're going to make you happy beyond belief," Toewi said, eyeing me with hunger in her eyes. "And when it's our turn to join in, I—"

"It'll come to that," Sekhmet said, giving her a look and then kneeling to remove my pants. The idea of a goddess kneeling before me was something, being surrounded by all these women as my hard cock leaped out, something else entirely. I was counting nine, unless my eyes were deceiving me. As aroused as my cock was, I felt a bit dizzy at the idea of pleasing them all, suddenly very nervous about my ability to do so.

"Go do your wives," Bastet said, her face transforming to that of a woman instead of a cat—though, interestingly and in a sexy way, her skin still had the spots of her cat form, her nose and eyes maintaining some of that look as well.

I nodded, feeling another surge of blood go to my cock, very aware of their eyes and hands on me as I stepped forward. Elisa let the last of her garments fall to the ground, exposing her cute little ass so that she was nude like the rest. She crawled onto the bed, letting Sharon take one of her nipples in her mouth, eyeing me, licking her lips.

A flood of energy swept over me and I turned to see the other ladies holding hands, waves of light moving my way. Each one felt like a warm bath that left me feeling both cleansed and amped up, as if there wasn't anything in the world that could stop me from making love to these ladies all night long.

Not wanting to waste another moment, I climbed onto the bed with my new wives, meeting Pucky for a kiss, then turning to kiss Red as Pucky moved her lips down my body, first to my chest and then my thighs. They pushed me back and Elisa kissed me while the others were running their hands along my skin, caressing my biceps, my chest, my abs. Tongues ran along my cock, the energy waves continuing in a way that brought new bliss to the whole encounter.

"How…?" I started, but Elisa put a finger to my lips, climbing on my cock first to ride me.

"Don't worry about the how from now on," she said. "There's no jealousy here, no reason to worry about offending one of us or anything like that."

She moaned, slapping her ass up and down on my legs as my cock filled her, then clenched and breathed heavily as she slid off and was met by Pucky diving in to go down on her. The heavy breathing increased, while Sharon pulled me up and had me go at her from behind. This position gave me a better view of my surroundings, and as my hips met her soft ass, cock sliding in, I noted the other ladies moving in, starting to caress each other again. They kept their distance from me until each of my wives had their chance.

After Sharon orgasmed, she moved over to kiss Bastet, hand clutching her ass with fervor, and Red grinned as she moved in for her turn with me.

"Having fun yet?" she asked.

My eyes went wide as I tried to figure out how to give the answer to that question justice. Instead of letting me try, she pressed her lips to mine, soft tongue playing with mine, and then she rolled me over so that I was on top, her legs up and on my shoulders as I slid my entire length into her. She opened her mouth as if to protest, but then bit down on her lip and nodded, encouraging me to bring my best. You can bet I did, rocking with her a good while as other orgasms initiated around me.

Then she climaxed and pushed me back to lick my thighs and balls, Pucky taking my shaft in her hand, eyes meeting mine.

"We love you," she said, and the other wives echoed it.

"And I love each of you," I said.

She pulled me off the bed and put one leg on it, so that I could make love to her while standing. A hand was on my ass and I turned to see Elisa there, her lips meeting my neck, then another hand was reaching between my legs, cupping my balls as I thrust, and I saw it was Sharon. Her eyes went wide as Red slid a finger into her ass, and the other ladies were on the bed now, watching and touching themselves, breathing heavily.

It hit me then that they were waiting with anticipation, knowing that this fuck with Pucky was the last one before they were apparently allowed to join in.

I was in no rush, but when Pucky thrust me back to the bed, muscles clenching and her voice going shrill as she screamed my name and said, "Oh, yes!" I had to admit, the anticipation added an extra layer of joy to it that sent a wave of bliss right through me.

So much so that suddenly my body convulsed, unable to hold back anymore, and I was coming along with Pucky. Our bodies were like one, both of us holding each other tight, moaning and kissing, until when she was done, she held her face close to mine, smiling wide.

"Oh," I said, finally glancing at the others and realizing what that meant. "Sorry."

"No need to apologize," Sekhmet said, and her

eyes went gold as another wave of light came over me as before.

I looked down to realize she was right. My cock was hard as ever, and as Toewi moved in to clean it off with her tongue, I had no doubt about being able to continue. Huera was there, beak and wings and all, and as sexy as she was I felt slightly confused about how that would work. At first it wasn't a concern, as Sekhmet and Bastet had more than earned their turn. Sekhmet shoved me back as Bastet purred and straddled me, letting me dive into her pussy. Meanwhile, I felt hands on my cock, a tongue, more mouths on my balls, and then Sekhmet, I assumed, was riding me.

Then it got a little weird, as Sekhmet got into it and grabbed hold of Bastet, nails digging into her. I didn't even notice until there was blood seeping down her chest from where the fingernails had dug into her shoulder. I started to pull away, to say something, but Bastet's eyes lit up and she reached back, digging her claws into my sides. My yelp was one of confused pain and pleasure, but… then I kind of got into it.

"Freaky," Elisa said with a chuckle.

"Just don't make it to the extent that Huera has to heal him," Red said.

I glanced over to see that most of them weren't

even going at it anymore, instead lounging about in each other's arms, watching. Another wave of pain hit me and suddenly my runes glowed. The action was a defensive one, something from my core, and I got why they were causing the pain. In addition to maybe simply liking it, my body and soul reacted in a way that sent me to new levels of vigor and sexuality. I couldn't take it passively anymore, throwing Bastet aside and plowing Sekhmet until she was shouting and punching me between her claw strikes, but I didn't care, I was loving it. She was spent, so I turned back to Bastet and lifted her onto me, turning her around as I did so that it was like she was sitting on my cock and I grabbed her breasts and wrapped an arm around her midsection, then started throwing her up and down on me as I grunted and fucked like I'd never fucked before.

Cheers came from the other ladies, though I wasn't sure if they were mocking me. I didn't care, and when Huera was at my side begging for a turn, Bastet mid-second orgasm, I was ready to give it to them all. I'd never fucked anything with wings before, but it worked easily enough to have her stand, grabbing her by the wings and doing her from behind, and then Toewi was on me, slamming me to the floor and moving her hips like a salsa queen at a dance contest, shaking them in ways I'd never thought applicable to sex but threatened to bring me to climax again. And it did—I was halfway there, feeling the throb in my cock before a knock came at the door and a guard started to say something as the door inched open.

In an flash, Roar was out and at the door, roaring loud with his wings spread. The guard probably pissed himself, he was gone so fast, running and shouting about needing a word.

"Fuck," Red said with a chuckle, then caressed my balls as she made for the door, grabbing her dress as she went. "I'll deal with it. Probably just Mowgli giving us a status update or something."

"Thanks," I said, then pushed back as Toewi thrust her hips into me, and I realized that in spite of her silence, she hadn't stopped, and had just orgasmed.

She fell back, sliding off my dick, and Sharon came forward.

"Ready for round two?" I asked.

"You bet your pretty cock I am," she said, but no sooner had she slid down onto me, *not* doggy style this time, eyes focused on mine intently… it hit, my body shaking, muscles clenching, and I came for the second time that night.

"Oh, my… god." I shook my head, watching the glow of the runes start to fade.

"Hey, you aren't done yet," Pucky said, caressing my cheek. Elisa was there too, biting my nipple playfully.

"We're going to drain you," she said.

I gulped, but sure enough, the pain made the runes glow again and I was ready. Fuck, right? To say each of them got a second go was an understatement, as some had three and four, and Red returned, confirming the guard hadn't had a real need for interrupting us, and when I came for the third time, this time Red taking it in the mouth, there was no doubt I was done.

Especially when, even with their surges of light, my dick simply refused to rise again. Hell, it was throbbing with heat anyway, and in need of a break. Judging by the sweaty, wild looks of the ladies, they'd had enough, too.

"To be clear," Elisa said as she reclined on the bed, causing her small breasts to rise and fall, "I could've gone all night."

"Sure, sure," Red said, wiping the edge of her mouth. "All of us could've but… I'm going to sleep."

In a few minutes, they were all starting to lie down, eyes closing, while a couple made their way to the bathroom to clean up. Huera for her part really did look like she could keep going, but she smiled pleasantly and followed me to one of the other bathrooms.

"Go first," I said, gesturing.

She cocked her head, clearly considering whether to say something. Finally, she muttered, "Thank you."

"For what?"

"Saving me, all of you. And… that, back there." She held out her wings. "It's gotta be weird, right? Fucking a bird."

"First, you're not a bird," I said, stepping close and wrapping an arm around her waist, one hand caressing the curve of one of her golden breasts. "You're a fairy tale, a Myth now… and beautiful. Fucking gorgeous."

"It's not weird? I mean…" Her eyes went a bit cross-eyed as she looked at her beak.

I shrugged. "It's also weird that there's a lioness and a cat back there, and it's really weird that a guy like me would end up with nine women at once. Fucking insane. And… all of it's amazing. AMAZING."

She chuckled. Took my hand and rubbed it along her cheek, then nodded and went into the bathroom without another word.

I considered waiting, but there were other bathroom's in the building. Making my way to the next closest one to clean myself, I glanced down and froze. What I saw scared the shit out of me. If Chris had thought his dick was swollen, mine was twice as bad, and looking about three times its normal girth. Impressive, but kind of scary. Running to find my clothes in the main entryway—yeah, a couple of guards gave me, and then my swollen dick, weird looks—I made my way to the bathroom.

I called Chris up.

"Remember that problem you had?" I asked.

"Don't need to bring up embarrassing shit."

"No, no… I just wanted to say—it apparently comes with the territory."

A pause, and then he laughed. "Dude, you telling me you got a case of the OC?"

"OC?"

"Yeah, man. Overworked cock."

I laughed. "Honestly, I'm surprised it's not rubbed raw the way they were going at it."

"Dude…" He paused, then said, "as soon as this honeymoon of yours is over, what'ya say to just getting together, having a pizza and some beers, and watching the Lord of the Rings trilogy straight through?"

"Maybe we take some breaks and get in some old school Secret of Mana playing?" I countered. "Throw that in, and you got yourself a deal."

"Done, but… let's do the next day."

"You have plans tomorrow?"

I thought about it, then said, "Yeah, actually. They ladies don't know it yet, but I'm going to take them out on a date. Maybe something simple and silly, like mini golf, or… I don't know, a bounce house."

He cracked up at that last one, reminding me where a bounce house would lead and how that was contrary to my idea of having a date and avoiding more OC for a bit.

"Good point," I replied with a chuckle. "Oh, a day cruise to Catalina?"

"Now you're talking. Let me know how it goes, so I can plan something like that soon, too."

"Not tomorrow? Double date?"

"Nah." He scoffed. "Me? I'm spending the day fucking—iced my dick and I think it's ready again."

"Perv." I chuckled. "All right, it's a deal. See you the day after tomorrow for some good nerdgasms."

"Deal."

I told him I looked forward to it, and hung up. After a quick rinse, I made my way back to the living room, where I found Pucky curled up on the couch next to Sharon. They gestured me over, and I plopped down between them, one arm around each.

"Everything okay?" Pucky asked.

"Aside from a crazy case of OC?" I asked.

She looked at me, confused, and I waved off the comment.

Leaning my head back, closing my eyes, and letting sleep start to take me, I said, "Life couldn't be more perfect."

THE END

So… how'd you like the final book in the Myth Protector trilogy? I hope it did what it promised! I set out to make a fun adventure with fairy tales, a guy's version of what we sometimes see in the romance realm. There's more to it—such as the Arthur thing, which actually started as a novel I was going to do about him as a vampire, and did it as a 'short story.' I'll give it away on Patreon and the newsletter, maybe? Something for me to figure out, as I'll likely finish it at some point. It was fun! But for now it's here for you all in this other format, so I feel content with it like that. What did you like about the series? What would you like to see more of? I'd love to hear!

NOTE: If you want the vampire short, sign up for

the newsletter and let me know. Likewise, if you want a scene with Chris first meeting his witches and having some spicy fun, same idea. (The latter might not be done yet, so patience please.)

Some ideas I'd originally considered having here actually ended up coming out in my series INTO THE RIFT, which started with RUNE WAKER. So if you're into stories with similarities to this, but without the fairy tale aspect, that might be a series you'd like to consider reading.

And if you want more... who knows! I like to finish story arcs in either three or four books, but that doesn't always mean a series is over for me. If another story idea hits me someday, maybe we'll come back to Jack and his high jinks. The guy has nine ladies now, though, so let's leave him alone for a bit so he can do his thing. He needs to figure out how to get over that OC situation, so he can be on continuous 'bring it' mode.

Thank you again for reading! I hope you get a chance to review, both in ebook and audio, and that you'll read my other stories.

Best,

Jamie Hawke

I'm super excited and hope you'll follow me on Facebook and Amazon (Click here and then 'Follow' under my name/pic). That way, you won't miss it! It's probably my best work ever.

Thank you again, and I look forward to hearing from you!

To connect directly:

https://www.facebook.com/groups/JamieHawke/

Also, for my GameLit Harem newsletter:

http://bit.ly/HaremGamelit

Do you want more Harem? I recommend this Facebook Group:

HaremGamelit Group

READ NEXT

Thank you for reading MYSTIC GUARDIANS!
Please consider laving a review on Amazon and
Goodreads. And don't miss out on the newsletter:

SIGN UP HERE

**And if you like this book, you might enjoy the Rift
Wars universe. Check out RUNE WAKER.**

***

Don't miss the bestseller SUPERS: EX HEROES.

Super powers. Super harem. Super awesome.

Contains Adult Content. Seriously.

Who in their right mind tells both his lawyer and the judge presiding over his murder trial, "Fuck you!" while still in the courtroom? No one, right? Yeah, you'd be wrong about that. I did.

You'd say the same thing if you were just found guilty of a murder you didn't commit, though. Call me crazy for going off like that in court, but trust me, you don't know crazy until you see what happened next.

I never believed in superheroes. I certainly didn't believe that I'd become one, or that strategically forming a harem of hot chicas and getting down with them to unlock my superpowers would be the key to my survival.

Did I say my survival? I meant the universe's. No, really...that's exactly what happened when I was taken to a galaxy of supers, thrown into a prison ship full of villains, and told it was up to me to stop them all.

Read on, friend, because it gets a whole hell of a lot crazier from here.

***

Want something a bit more insane? Planet Kill is like Battle Royale on a planet with Gamelit elements... and it's crazy. You'll see - You can grab book one and two on Amazon!

Grab PLANET KILL now!

Form your harem. Kill or be killed. Level up and loot. Welcome to Planet Kill.

Pierce has his mission: survive by killing and getting nasty, doing whatever it takes to find his lost wife and others who were abducted and forced to participate in the barbarity that is Planet Kill. In a galaxy where the only way to rise up in society and make it to the paradise planets is through this insanity, he will be up against the most desperate, the most ruthless, and the sexiest fighters alive.

Because it's not just a planet--it's the highest rated show around. Contestants level up for kills, get paid for accepting violent and sexual bids, and factions have been made in the form of harems.

His plan starts to come together when he meets Letha, one of the most experienced warlords on the planet. She's as lethal as they come and a thousand times as sexy. He's able to learn under her, to start to form his own harem.

Only, being her ally means fighting her wars.

It's kill or be killed, level up fast and put on the show the viewers want all while proving to Letha and her generals that he has what it takes to be one of them. The alternative is death, leaving his wife to her fate of being hunted by monsters.

MY OTHER WORKS: JUSTIN SLOAN

You also might want to read the stuff I write that isn't harem/ spicy sauce stuff. If so, you'll want to head over to the Justin Sloan books. Here they are!

Books by Justin Sloan

SCIENCE FICTION

ASCENSION GATE (Space Opera with Dragon
Shifters and Vampires)
Star Forged
(More coming soon!)

BIOTECH WARS (Space Station Genetic
Engineering)
Project Destiny ($0.99)
Project Exodus
Project Ascent

VALERIE'S ELITES (Vampires in Space -
Kurtherian Gambit Universe 4 Book Series)
Valerie's Elites
Death Defied
Prime Enforcer
Justice Earned

RECLAIMING HONOR (Vampires and
Werewolves - Kurtherian Gambit Universe 8
Book Series, Complete)
Justice is Calling
Claimed by Honor
Judgment has Fallen
Angel of Reckoning
Born into Flames
Defending the Lost

Return of Victory

Shadow Corps (Space Opera Fantasy/ Light LitRPG - Seppukarian Universe 3 Book Series, Complete)

Shadow Corps

Shadow Worlds

Shadow Fleet

War Wolves (Space Opera Fantasy - Seppukarian Universe 3 Book Series, Complete)

Bring the Thunder

Click Click Boom

Light Em Up

Syndicate Wars (Space Marines and Time Travel - Seppukarian Universe 5 Book Series, Complete)

First Strike

The Resistance

Fault Line

False Dawn

Empire Rising

FANTASY

The Hidden Magic Chronicles (Epic Fantasy -

Kurtherian Gambit Universe 4 Book Series,
Complete)
Shades of Light
Shades of Dark
Shades of Glory
Shades of Justice

FALLS OF REDEMPTION (Epic Fantasy Series 4
Book Series)
Land of Gods (NOW FREE!)
Retribution Calls
Tears of Devotion

MODERN NECROMANCY (Supernatural Thriller
3 Book Series, Complete)
Death Marked
Death Bound
Death Crowned

CURSED NIGHT
Hounds of God

ALLIE STROM (MG Urban Fantasy Trilogy 3
Book Series, Complete)
Allie Strom and the Ring of Solomon (Now FREE!)
Allie Strom and the Sword of the Spirit
Allie Strom and the Tenth Worthy

17603794R00187